HEAT
of the
NIGHT

By Sylvia Day

HEAT OF THE NIGHT
PLEASURES OF THE NIGHT
ALLURING TALES (ANTHOLOGY)

Coming Soon

ALLURING TALES 2 (ANTHOLOGY)

Heat
of the
Night

Sylvia Day

red

AVON

An Imprint of HarperCollins*Publishers*

To my family, who have been so tremendously supportive of my career with nary a complaint about how much I work/write. Releasing nine books in one year takes a lot out of a writer, and they paid the price with such grace and love.

Thank you for embracing my dream and adjusting your lives to suit it. There are no words to express how much that means to me. You give me strength.

I love you.

HEAT OF THE NIGHT. Copyright © 2008 by Sylvia Day. All rights reserved. Printed in the United States of America. No part of this book may be used or reproduced in any manner whatsoever without written permission except in the case of brief quotations embodied in critical articles and reviews. For information address HarperCollins Publishers, 10 East 53rd Street, New York, NY 10022.

HarperCollins books may be purchased for educational, business, or sales promotional use. For information please write: Special Markets Department, HarperCollins Publishers, 10 East 53rd Street, New York, NY 10022.

FIRST EDITION

Designed by Elizabeth M. Glover

Library of Congress Cataloging-in-Publication Data

Day, Sylvia.
    Heat of the night / Sylvia Day. —1st ed.
       p. cm — (Dream guardians; #2)
    ISBN: 978-0-06-123103-2
    1. Dreams—Fiction.   I. Title.
PS3604.A9875H43   2008
813'.6—dc22
                2007039197

    12   OV/RRD   10 9 8 7 6 5 4 3 2

Acknowledgments

Thanks go out to my critique partner, Annette McCleave (www.AnnetteMcCleave.com), who helped me find the focus of the beginning of this book.

Hugs go out to fabulous authors and dear friends Renee Luke, Sasha White, and Jordan Summers who were there on the other side of the IM window when I needed someone to listen, commiserate, and give me a swift kick in the @ss.

To my sister, Samara Day, who puts up with me and my aversion to talking on the phone.

You are one of the precious lights in my life, Sam. I have loved you with all my heart from the day you were born. As you've grown into a woman I admire and respect, I only love you more. You are a blessing I am grateful for every day.

*Beware of the Key that opens the Lock
and reveals the Truth.*

# Chapter 1

The Twilight

Connor Bruce took out the nearest guard with a perfectly aimed blow dart.

It was a split-second assault, but the tranquilizer took a bit longer to work than that. The guard had time to yank the dart free and withdraw his glaive before his eyes rolled back into his head and he collapsed to the floor in a puddle of red garments.

"Sorry, chap," Connor muttered, as he bent over the fallen body and collected the guard's comm unit and sword. The man would awake with only the vague sensation of having dozed, perhaps in boredom.

Connor straightened and whistled a low warbling birdcall, telling Lieutenant Philip Wager that he'd succeeded in his task. The responding whistle told him the other Temple guards around the perimeter had also been neutralized. Within moments he was surrounded by a dozen of his men. They were dressed for battle in dark gray, form-fitting sleeveless tunics and matching loose pants. Connor wore similar garments, but his were black denoting his rank as Captain of the Elite Warriors.

"You're going to see things inside that will startle you," Connor warned, his blade whistling as he pulled it free of its scabbard on his back. "Focus on the mission. We have to figure out how the Elders brought Captain Cross back to the Twilight from the Dreamers' plane of existence."

"Yes, Captain."

Wager aimed a pulse emitter at the massive red *torii* gate that herald the entrance to the Temple complex, temporarily disturbing the vid unit that recorded those who visited. Connor stared at the archway with a roiling mixture of horror, confusion, and anger. The structure was so imposing it forced every Guardian to stare and read the warning engraved in the ancient language—*"Beware of the Key that turns the Lock."*

For centuries, he and every member of his team had hunted the Dreamer who was prophesied to come to their world through the dream state and destroy them. The Dreamer who would see them as they were and recognize that they were not a figment of a nocturnal imagination, but real beings who lived in the Twilight—the place where the human mind came in slumber.

But Connor had already met the infamous Key and she wasn't a specter of doom and annihilation. She was a slender-but-curvy blonde veterinarian with big dark eyes and a deep well of compassion.

Lies, all of it. All these years wasted. Luckily for the Key—also known innocuously as Lyssa Bates—Captain Aidan Cross, warrior of legend and Connor's best friend, had found her first. Found her, fell in love with her, and eloped with her to the mortal plane.

Now it was Connor's mission to unravel the mysteries of the Elders here in the Twilight, and everything he needed to know was safeguarded in the Temple of the Elders.

Let's go, he mouthed.

With the timing down to pinpoint accuracy, they rushed through the gate. They split into two teams running along either side of the stone-lined center courtyard, weaving in and out among fluted columns of alabaster stone.

The wind blew gently, carrying with it the fragrance of nearby flowers and fields of wild grass. It was the time of day when the Temple was closed to the general public and the Elders were secluded in meditation. The perfect time to break in and steal whatever information and secrets they could get their hands on.

Connor entered the *haiden* first. Holding up three fingers, he then waved to the right while he moved to the left. Three Elites obeyed the silent command and took the east side of the circular room.

The two teams moved within the shadows, highly aware that any misstep would allow the vid units around the perimeter to pick up their incursion. In the center of the vast space waited semicircular rows of benches that faced the columned entryway they had just come through. Rising several stories high, there were so many benches the Guardians had lost count of the number of Elders who ruled from them long ago. This was the heart of their world, the center of law and order. The seat of power.

Regrouping at the middle hallway that led to the *honden,* Connor paused, and the others awaited his command.

The hall to the west branched off toward the Elders' living quarters. The hall to the right went to a secluded open-air meditation courtyard.

This center gallery was where it got freaky. After his first—and heretofore only—Temple break-in, he was prepared. His men weren't.

He looked at them with an arched brow, silently admonishing them to heed his earlier command. They nodded grimly, and Connor continued on.

As they walked, a vibration beneath their feet drew everyone's attention to the floor. The stone shimmered and became translucent, creating the impression that the ground had disintegrated and they were about to fall into an endless blanket of stars. He groped for the wall by instinct, his teeth gritted together, then the view of space melted into a swirling kaleidoscope of colors.

"Fuck me," Wager breathed.

Connor had said the exact same thing the first time he'd walked this corridor. Every step created ripples in the colors, suggesting that whatever it was responded to their presence.

"Is that real?" Corporal Trent whispered fiercely. "Or a hologram of some sort?"

Lifting his hand, Connor reminded the men to keep their silence. He had no idea what the damn thing was. He knew only that he couldn't look at it or vertigo would make him sick.

They moved past the private Elder library to reach the control room. There was one Elder there, a lone sentinel lost within a vast space dominated by high walls lined with bound volumes and a large console. As was the custom of the Elders, he'd been left behind when the others retired for the afternoon, which made him the unfortunate recipient of a tranq dart to the neck. Connor dragged his unconscious body aside to give Wager access to the crescent-shaped touchpad control panel.

"I'll loop the vids so you're not recorded," the lieutenant said.

Wager stepped up and began to work, his posture straight and legs slightly parted, firmly entrenched in his assignment. With his long black hair and stormy gray eyes, he had a renegade appearance to go along with his loose-cannon reputation. Because of his volatile nature, he'd been a second lieutenant for centuries longer than he should have been. Connor had recently promoted him to first lieutenant, for all the good that did him. They were insurgents, having left the sanctioned Elite Warrior regiments to commandeer the rebel faction.

Confident in Wager's ability to manage the database part of their search, Connor stationed two lookouts by the entrance and took two men with him to perform a physical search of the premises. Not long ago, he'd broken into the Temple with only Wager as backup. But the recent coup had forced the Elders to increase the number of guards, which in turn forced Connor to charge the complex with a dozen men. Six outside and six inside.

They moved with rapid strides further down the hallway, keeping their gazes averted from the rapidly swirling kaleidoscopic floor. Light poured in from the skylights above and a clear door at the end of the hall provided a sunlit view of the far edge of the meditation courtyard.

As they reached a doorway, Connor gestured one man inside. "Anything unusual."

The man nodded and stepped into the doorless room with glaive drawn and at the ready. Connor repeated the process with the second soldier until he was continuing on alone. He took the next room he came across.

It was a dark space, not unusual since it was unoccupied, but odd in that the lighting did not illuminate when he entered. It was only the light spilling in from the hallway that enabled him to see.

The center of the room was empty, but tiered metal carts on wheels lined the walls. There was a medicinal smell in the air and as he spotted a heavy bolted metal door in the wall, his hackles rose. There was a thick viewing window built into the upper part of the massive barrier, but whether that was for someone to see in or someone to see out, he didn't know. Either way, that door was a serious deterrent and meant that whatever it guarded was important.

"What the hell have you got in there?" he wondered aloud.

Connor stepped over to the small touchpad in the corner and began a rapid fire series of keystrokes. He needed to get the damn lights to turn on so he could see what the hell he was dealing with. He could use some leverage right now, and holding a valuable item for ransom would work nicely.

One of the many command overrides he inputted caused the panel to beep rapidly and then the room slowly brightened.

"Yes!" He grinned and turned around, surveying the small room with its stone floor and barren white walls.

The sharp hiss of releasing hydraulic pressure had him rocking back on the heels of his boots. Somehow he'd managed to get the door open, too, which made things all the easier.

What happened next would forever be ingrained on Connor's memory. There was a roar that sounded like fury mixed with fear, then the heavy door flew open with such explosive force that it embedded into the adjacent wall.

His glaive at the ready, Connor was prepared to fight. What he wasn't prepared for was the apparition that lunged at him, a body seemingly Guardian-like in appearance, yet possessed of pure black eyes with no sclera and teeth with wickedly sharp points.

Connor froze, horrified and confused. It was the gravest offense to kill another Guardian and to his knowledge murder hadn't been committed in centuries. That stayed his hand when he would have thrust, which left him open to the violent impact that knocked him to the floor. A feat never before accomplished because he was too damn big.

"Fuck!" he grunted as he crashed to the stone with bone-jarring force.

The thing was on top of him, a not-inconsiderable male filled with unexplained ferocity. It was snarling and grappling like a rabid beast. Connor jerked to the side, rolling to gain the upper hand. With one hand wrapped around his assailant's straining neck and the other fisting and descending in brutal punches, he should have knocked the man out cold. He felt the crack of a cheekbone beneath his knuckles and the shattering of a nose, but the injuries appeared to have no effect, neither did the deprivation of air to breathe.

Deep inside Conner, fear curled with insidious strength. Those black eyes where filled with a roiling madness and thick claws were ripping at the skin of his forearms. How did one defeat an enemy who had no mind?

"Captain!"

Connor didn't look up. He rolled onto his back again and extended his arm full-length, holding his attacker aloft by the throat. A glaive whistled through the air and sliced off the top of the man's skull. Gore splattered everywhere.

"What the fuck was that?" Trent cried, standing just above Connor's head with the killing blade in his hands.

"Hell if I know." Connor tossed the body off to the side. He looked down at himself in disgust, touching the gunk that coated him with a tentative finger. It was thick and black, resembling old blood and reeking like it, too. His gaze moved to the corpse whose face from the eyebrows down was still intact. Brown hair grew overly long around the man's ears and nape. The skin had an unhealthy pallor and the flesh was clinging to bones. The hands and feet were both capped with long, thick, reptilian claws. But it was the inky black, sightless eyes and gaping maw that were so frightening. They turned a gaunt, sickly looking man into a formidable predator.

It wore only loose white pants that were stained and torn. On the back of its hand was a seared brand—"HB-12." A quick look at the cell from which it escaped revealed a thick metal interior liberally gouged.

"Your room is definitely more interesting than mine," Trent said. The levity of his statement was ruined by the crack in his voice.

Connor's chest labored more from his anger than from

his exertions. "It's exactly this sort of shit that forced the rebellion!"

Most everyone would say that leading a revolt went against his easygoing nature, and they'd be right. Hell, he still had trouble believing he'd taken this step. But there were too many goddamn questions and all the answers he had were lies. Yeah, he was a man who liked things painfully simple—*wine, women, and kicking ass*, as he used to say—but he had no qualms about stepping up to the plate and swinging when necessary.

It was his job to protect others, both Dreamers and the gentler Guardians. There were thousands of his people, all were divided into certain specialties. Each Guardian had their strengths. Some were tender and offered comfort to Dreamers who grieved. Others were playful and filled in dreams of sports heroes or baby showers. There were Sensuals and Healers, Nurturers and Challengers. Connor was an Elite. He killed Nightmares and guarded his people. If he had to protect them from the Elders, too, so be it.

"There's no way to pretend that the Temple wasn't breached now," the corporal pointed out.

"Nope," Connor agreed, "no way." And he didn't really care at this point. In fact, he wanted the Elders to know that their secrets weren't safe. He wanted them looking over their shoulders. He wanted them to feel as unsettled and wary as he did. They owed him that much, at least, after asking him to lay his life on the line for a fake cause.

Wager came running into the room with two more Elite directly behind him. "Whoa!" he said, skidding in the splatter before catching his footing. "What the hell is *that*?"

"Fuck if I know." Connor wrinkled his nose.

"Yeah," Wager agreed. "It stinks. It's also probably what set off the alarm on the console. My guess is reinforcements are on their way now, so we better get out of here."

"Did we get anything useful out of the database?" Connor asked, grabbing a towel off one of the push carts against the wall. He scrubbed at his torn skin and clothes to remove what he could of the blood-like substance clinging to him.

"I downloaded what I could. It would take eons to get all of it, but I tried to focus on files that sounded the most intriguing."

"That will have to suffice. Let's go."

They left with the same caution they'd used upon their arrival, their eyes scanning their surroundings carefully. Still, none of them saw the Elder whose dark gray robes blended so well with the shadows.

He stood silent and unnoticed. Smiling.

Chapter 2

"Where's Lieutenant Wager?" Connor asked, glancing around the main underwater cavern, which served as headquarters for the rebel faction in the Twilight.

Above their heads, hundreds of tiny vid screens flashed various scenes like movies, glimpses into the open minds of thousands of "Mediums"—Dreamers brought here without sleep. They hovered in the Twilight, more awake than not, but lacking full comprehension.

The humans called the process of forcibly inducing subconscious thought "hypnosis." Whatever name one gave to it, their destination was this cavern. Here the Elders had watched over them and prevented the Nightmares from using their stream of subconscious to reach the mortal plane.

"In the back, sir," replied the Elite warrior standing guard at the mouth of the pool, the only physical entrance or exit.

With a nod of acknowledgment, Connor turned on

his heel and strode the length of the rock-lined hallway. Carved into the very heart of the mountain, it seemed to have no end and was disorienting with its matching arched doorways on either side. Thousands of them. All filled with glass tubes, which held Elders-in-training in stasis of some sort. His men had yet to discern who the occupants were, or why they were being kept in that manner.

Frankly, Connor thought the whole thing was creepy, and he was shaken by the realization that he'd lived centuries never knowing anything about his world or the Elders who ruled it. It made him sick to think of how stubborn he'd been when Aidan asked him to consider everything that was unexplained. He had refused to see the signs that bothered his friend for so long.

Connor's boot steps echoed rhythmically as he traversed the distance to his second-in-command with a rapid, agitated stride. Soon the sounds from the largest room faded into silence. Sadly, using "large" to describe the size was only possible when comparing the room to the others down here.

The space was actually pretty damn small, having been designed for the comfortable occupation of only three Elders-in-training. The main cavern was cramped by a half-moon console and the massive screen of rapidly flickering images. Depending on one's angle, a Guardian could see right through the display into the room beyond, a space filled with slipstreams—wide beams of moving light that represented streams of subconscious thought.

Snorting, Connor acknowledged for the millionth time that he still didn't quite grasp the whole concept of the

Twilight. Aidan had badgered their teacher at the Elite Academy with endless questions about where they'd come from and where they now were. The simplest explanation Connor had heard was that he should think of the Twilight like an apple. Abbreviated space is the hole bored through the center by a worm, or a "wormhole." Instead of coming out the other side though, the Elders found a way to suspend the Guardians inside. They called that pocket the Twilight. Connor called it confusing.

"Wager!" he roared, as he passed through one of the arched doorways and found the lieutenant engrossed at a console.

The younger man jumped, then glared. "You scared the crap out of me!"

"Sorry."

"No, you're not."

Connor grinned. "No. I'm not. I had my share of scares today. It's your turn."

Shaking his head, Wager pushed to his feet and stretched his tall, wiry frame. "It's good to see you smiling." He crossed his arms and stood with widespread legs. He was a handsome lad, with an appeal the female Guardians described as "bad boy."

Women. They loved trouble.

"There's not a whole hell of a lot to smile about. Some freak of nature attacked me today, my best friend has run off with the Key, and I need to get laid."

Wager threw his head back and laughed. "I bet the ladies are missing you, too. I've heard poems are written about your stamina and on Girls' Night Out they compare notes."

"No way."

"Yes, way. Morgan calls you the 'golden god with the golden rod.'"

Connor felt his face heat and ran a self-conscious hand through his slightly too-long blond hair. "You're full of shit. She wouldn't say that to you."

Black brows rose. "Morgan?"

A mental image of the dark-eyed slender Player Guardian entered Connor's thoughts. His lips curved ruefully. "Yeah, I suppose she might."

"First Cross takes off, now you're in exile . . . I bet there's more than a few broken hearts."

"You're a popular guy yourself."

"I have my charms," the lieutenant drawled.

"Sometimes when I'm waiting for Cross to connect to the Twilight, I look over the rise at the Dreamers' slipstreams and seriously think about hopping into one. If only for a half hour or so."

Wager's merriment faded into the intensity that made him a damn good warrior. "How is Captain Cross's stream? Is it coming in clearer yet?"

"No." Connor scratched the back of his neck. "It's still murky. I'm guessing that has something to do with the fact that his slipstream connects to that barren plain instead of in the Valley."

For most Dreamers, their subconscious connected to the Twilight in the Valley of Dreams. They touched the lives of Guardians through wide golden beams that rose from the valley floor and pierced the misty sky until they could no longer be seen. The varying streams of subconscious thoughts spread as far as the eye could see.

"Actually, I think that's a manifestation of the problem,

not the cause." At Connor's raised brow, Wager explained. "Because we are physiologically different from humans, I suspect our brain waves function on another wavelength entirely. That's what causes Cross's slipstream to connect to the Twilight in a different place and to come across with a degraded intensity."

When Aidan entered the dream state, he came to them in a blue stream. While the other slipstreams where clear enough to look through—almost like looking through a thin waterfall—Aidan came across *snowy*, like a television station with bad reception.

"Okay." Connor heaved out his breath. "That puts a new spin on things."

"Sure does."

"Corporal Trent said you had some news for me?"

"Yes." Wager rolled his shoulders back as if to relieve strain.

Connor's hackles rose. "Lemme guess. It's not good."

"Using information gleaned from the data chips I loaded in the Temple, I found a reference to 'HB-9.'"

"That thing in the Temple was branded with 'HB-12.'"

"I saw that." The lieutenant's lips pursed grimly. "Unfortunately, the file containing the information on the HB Project was incomplete, because the download was aborted too soon."

"Shit." Connor scowled. *"HB Project?* What does that mean?"

"It means that thing was part of a greater program, but I can't tell how extensive it was."

"Fuck." Connor felt like hitting something. "If there are more of those freaks, we've got problems."

"That's putting it mildly."

"I have to warn Cross."

"Yes." Wager nodded sagely. "And because he doesn't remember what you tell him in dreams, you'll have to do it in person."

"What?" Connor gaped. "Are you nuts?"

"You've seen one of those things," the lieutenant pointed out, "and fought with it. That gives you an advantage. Trent's the only other Elite who saw it in action and you know he's not ready for a mission such as this."

Connor growled and began to pace the length of the stone-walled room.

"Think about it, captain. Do you trust anyone else to relay the gravity of this situation to Cross? I don't."

"I trust you."

Wager stilled, then cleared his throat. "Thank you, sir. I appreciate that, you know I do. But you need me here going through the entries we downloaded from the database, and you and Captain Cross have a unique dynamic. For centuries you have kept the Elite in tight fighting form with high morale and a low casualty rate. And you're friends. I think in a new world, possibly fighting a new enemy you're going to need that support to succeed."

"It's a bad idea to send the highest ranking officer away from the troops. I don't like it. Not one bit." Connor glanced at the Elder-in-training who slept oblivious in the nearby glass tube. His head hung low, his chin to his chest, his body held upright by no discernable device. This one was dark-haired and very young. Not much past his teens Connor would guess.

"I don't like it either, but here are the facts: I'm the best person to search the database and you are the best person to work with Cross. By reversing that, we would be crippling both missions before they start. We can't afford to do that."

"Damn it, I know that." Connor scrubbed both hands through his hair. "I'm not even really arguing the point. It's just the principle of the thing that gets to me."

"I understand that you're not arguing. I know I'm only saying aloud the thoughts you have in your head. Frankly, I wish I could be the one to go." Wager smiled, his gray eyes lit with wry amusement. "I've got a Dreamer of my own I'd like to track down."

"No way."

Wager shrugged. "But you're the one who should go. I'm more than capable of running things around here."

"I know." Connor heaved out his breath. "You should have been promoted a long time ago."

"I don't know about that," the lieutenant said easily. "My emotions get in the way more than they should. I'm growing out of it, but it's taken me a few centuries."

Connor turned toward the open archway. "I'll go speak to the men. You find me a Medium in Southern California."

"Captain?" Wager called after him.

"Yes?"

"About coming back . . ."

Jaw tensing, Connor raised both brows in silent query.

"I discovered something else. When we physically ride a human's stream of subconscious thought, we leave a traceable thread behind. It can then be used to 'yank' the Guardian back."

"That's how the Elders brought Aidan back?"

"Apparently. If necessary, we can pull you back the same way. But . . . the Medium is damaged in the process."

"Damaged?"

"It's fatal to humans." The lieutenant crossed his arms and settled more firmly on his heels, a stance Connor had come to recognize as preparation for a difficult task. "Strokes, dilated cardiomyopathy . . . 'sudden deaths' are the result."

"Shit." Connor reached out to the threshold of the archway and leaned his weight into it. "That's why it's not a viable means of hopping between the two planes."

"I suspect that's the reason we haven't migrated over there," Wager agreed, "if only in small numbers. We would have to leave guards behind to prevent the Nightmares from using the slipstreams. No battalion would want that assignment indefinitely and we'd have to leave at least that many behind to stem the flow of Nightmares from the Gateway and guard the Valley."

"But we couldn't relieve them because traveling back and forth would kill thousands of Mediums."

"Right."

Every Guardian understood their responsibility. Their homeworld had been invaded by Nightmares, a race of shadowy evanescent parasites. The Elders had created a fissure within abbreviated space. It had served as a portal to this conduit plane between the human dimension and the one the Guardians had been forced to leave behind. The Nightmares had quickly followed, forcing their way past a formidable barrier—the Gateway—and hundreds of

Elite Warriors. "We screwed up by letting the Nightmares in. We can't compound the problem by killing them ourselves or taking over their world."

Nodding grimly, Connor's gaze moved around the room, his brain attempting to wrap around his departure. He may never see this place again. A few minutes ago, that would have been lovely. Now he felt adrift. He smelled the mustiness of damp air and felt the coarse rock beneath his palm, but the sensations didn't ground him. He felt completely unanchored. "I understand. We need the humans alive."

"Yes, for our sense of obligation but also for our own survival. We would top off their food chain, disrupting the order of predation. Over time, they could become extinct and killing of an entire link would have potentially annihilatory effects on Earth. That in turn could ripple outward across their galaxy and beyond. We could see a—"

"Whoa!" Connor grumbled, lifting his hands in a defensive gesture. "Brain overload. I get the idea."

"Sorry."

"Don't be. We'll get through this. The Elite always do." Straightening, Connor inhaled deeply and fixed his mind on his task. "Find me a Medium in Southern California. I'll get ready and explain the mission to the others."

"Yes, sir." Wager saluted.

Connor returned the gesture, then spun about and left.

Connor stared at the streams of golden light and inhaled deeply into his lungs. He reminded himself that Aidan made this very same journey just weeks ago. If he could do it, so could Connor.

But Cross wasn't happy here, whispered a voice in his mind. Connor was. He'd always been content.

"Are you ready, Captain?"

He glanced through the glass monitor at the console where Wager worked and nodded grimly.

"The stream directly to your right will take you to a Medium in Anaheim, California, which is about an hour from Temecula where Captain Cross is living with Lyssa Bates."

"Got it."

"These slipstreams work differently from those of Dreamers." Wager leaned back in his chair, his features tight with strain. Long strands of his black hair escaped from his queue, his exterior so at odds with his almost bookish nature. He looked more like a Hell's Angel biker than he did a computer geek. "They are in motion. You will leap into their subconscious and find yourself riding it into their plane of existence. Your appearance there will cause a temporal disturbance, which will affect a hitch in time."

"A hitch?" Connor frowned.

"Yeah, a major slowing down. A second to them will be like a minute to you. I'm not sure how that will feel. Not good, I'm guessing. But if you hurry, it will allow you to leave without being detected. Otherwise, for the humans, one second you won't be there and the next second you will. That'll be hard to explain, so I wouldn't push my luck if I were you."

"No problem. I'll get out of way quick."

"I'll be able to track you through your dreams, just as you've been meeting Captain Cross in dreams."

Connor gave him a thumbs-up. It was the best he could do under the circumstances. His throat was too tight to speak.

Despite his many centuries of living, for the most part he felt not much older than he'd been when he graduated from the Elite Academy with Aidan. Sure, he could no longer fuck all night and tear up Nightmares the next day without feeling like rubber. But that was more of a dig to his male pride, than it was a sign of his age.

Right now, though, he felt every one of his years.

Wager heaved out his breath. "I admire you greatly, Bruce. I think I'm more nervous than you are."

"Nah. I'm just hiding it better." He turned to face the appropriate slipstream. His glaive was strapped to his back and he wore a clean uniform. He was as ready as he would ever be. "See you on the other side," he said.

Then he jumped.

Wild beasts were ripping off his limbs and pounding his skull into a rock.

At least that's the way it felt to Connor as he slowly came to a vague sense of awareness. It took all the energy he had just to lift his head. Getting his eyes open was nearly impossible. Blinking, he tried to focus on where he was.

It was dark except for the multicolored tiny lights glowing in the night sky. The smell that filled his nostrils was intense, overpowering. Musky, smoky, nauseating. Connor felt his stomach lurch, then roil. His skull was gripped in a closing vice. His teeth ached. The roots of his hair stung and burned.

He was dying. No one could feel like this much shit and live. It wasn't possible.

Connor's brain stumbled into painful thought, goaded by sheer survival instinct.

. . . one second you won't be there and the next second you will . . . that'll be hard to explain . . .

He wasn't sure there was anyone to explain to. From the looks of it, he'd ridden a slipstream straight into a hell dimension. The stench in the air was just a few breaths away from making him vomit.

Heaving his torso upward, Connor managed a kneeling position and then pushed back to rest on his heels. Everything around him spun dizzily. He groaned in misery and clutched his waist.

"Fuck me."

He glanced around with gritty eyes. Slowly, his surroundings came into focus. A thin line of light beckoned and Connor reached out for it . . . and promptly fell back into an ignoble sprawl. It was a curtain and he tugged it out of the way to find a massive convention hall. People stood nearby, impossibly close, frozen in a single moment in time.

It was a science fiction convention of some sort. Some of the attendees were heavily disguised in costumes that ranged from alien beings to robots.

Looking over his shoulder, Connor surveyed the room he was in. He was in a small makeshift tent of some sort. Everything was black. The floor was hard and cold, but covered in a rough tarp. There was a round table nearby draped in black material. Atop it was a globe, which was creating the light reflecting off what he now realized was a ceiling. A woman lay on a padded table, eyes closed, lost in the hypnotic state that had brought him here. Connor suspected she had been "put under" by the man presently bent over stealing money from her purse.

Snorting with disgust, Connor lurched to unsteady feet and tried not to breathe through his nose. He withdrew the man's wallet out of his back pocket and took all the cash from inside.

"Karma, asshole."

He left as quickly as his shaky legs would allow. There was a soft buzzing in the air, the sound of words forming in their most infantile states. How he made it through the crowds was a mystery to him. The scents of the human world assaulted him. Fake smells, such as perfumes. Food smells. Body odor.

In the Twilight and in the Dreamers' subconscious such sensory perceptions were dulled or stripped to their most basic. Not so in reality. Connor was forced to pause at a trash receptacle by the exit to throw up.

He didn't like it here. His heart ached. He wanted to go home, a home he loved and missed terribly already.

Instead he pushed open the glass doors of the Anaheim Convention Center and stepped out to his new world.

Stacey Daniels knew it was ridiculous to be sitting on the couch bawling her eyes out. She should be thrilled to have some personal time for herself.

"I should be making an appointment for a pedicure, a manicure, and a haircut," she muttered.

She should be calling the hot UPS driver who delivered the pharmaceutical supplies to Bates' All Creatures Animal

Hospital where she worked. He'd given her his card with his cell phone number on it after weeks of flirting. The accompanying wink had made the offer more than just a business one.

"I could be looking forward to a night of much-needed, no-strings-attached raunchy sex." She sniffled. "Hell, I could be *having* raunchy sex, right now."

Instead, she was a miserable lump, crying because her deadbeat ex-boyfriend had finally picked up their son for an overdue weekend visit. It was pitiful and slightly deranged, but she couldn't get over it.

Sinking deeper into her best friend's sofa, Stacey looked around the condo and was grateful to be house-sitting for her boss, Lyssa Bates. She didn't know how she would have managed being at her own home without Justin there. It would be too lonely. At least Lyssa had fish and a cat, though Jelly Bean was the meanest cat ever. A grumpy, hissing, tail-flicking beast who was presently sitting on the arm of the couch giving her the evil eye. Still, even his unpleasant company was better than being alone.

Of course, Stacey was realizing exactly how lonely she really was. At some point she'd stopped seeing herself as an individual woman and started herself only as "Justin's mom," which wasn't healthy, as her reaction this morning so aptly proved. She had no idea what to do with herself. How sad was that?

You have a right to be mad, the devil on her shoulder said.

She worked her ass off to make ends meet without a dime of child support and Tommy was the one who got to take Justin skiing for his first time. Tommy got to be "cool." Tommy got the privilege of seeing Justin's face light up with joy and wonder. All because he'd had a twenty-dollar bill burning a hole in his pocket in Reno a year ago. A twenty he'd promptly put down as a bet that the Colts would go to the Super Bowl.

"A twenty he should have paid *me*," she bitched, "so I could put gas in the car to get to work and support *our* child."

It was so unfair. She had been saving up for a getaway to Big Bear for almost two years and Tommy ripped it out from under her in two minutes. Just like her life had been ripped out from under her when she'd gotten pregnant in college. *You can always abort,* he'd said blithely. *We've got our whole lives ahead of us and years of school. You can't have a baby.*

"Asshole," she griped. She'd had to drop out of school and get government assistance. Tommy had said it was her choice and good luck. See ya, wouldn't wanna be ya. He'd gone on to graduate and became a struggling screenwriter who had enough money to party, but not for child support. She'd gone on to a series of temp jobs until she finally found steady, good-paying, nondemeaning work at the vet hospital with Lyssa.

Stacey yanked a tissue from the box next to her and blew her nose. It was petty and small of her to begrudge Justin a much-wanted trip just because she wasn't the one to take him. She knew it and acknowledged it, but doing so didn't make her feel any better.

The doorbell rang and Stacey turned her head to scowl in the direction of the foyer. If she'd been at home, she would have ignored it, but she was watching Lyssa's house and pets while the boss was on a mini-vacation with her fiancé in Mexico, so that meant watching out for Lyssa's packages, too.

Grumbling under her breath, Stacey stood and crossed the soothing beige carpeted living room to the marble-lined entrance hall. JB hissed and followed her, rumbling his demon cat's warning. He hated visitors. Well, he hated everybody pretty much, but especially total strangers.

The bell rang again, impatiently, and she called out, "Hang on! I'm getting there."

Stacey turned the knob and pulled the door open. "You gotta give a girl a minute to get—"

A Viking stood on Lyssa's porch.

And he was devastatingly gorgeous.

Chapter 3

JB's bitching halted mid-rumble, just as Stacey's speech had.

Gaping, she took a long, hard look at the blond giant who filled every inch of the doorway. He was at least six foot four, with a sword hilt peeking over his left shoulder and a brawny chest that would make Dwayne "The Rock" Johnson jealous. His arms were massive, ripped with taut muscles that stretched the golden skin covering them. He wore a straight black, sleeveless v-neck tunic that looked painted on and pants that clung to lean hips before flowing into loose pants legs. On his feet he sported wicked-looking combat boots.

"Wowza," she murmured, duly impressed. The man was hot, hot, hot. Even in a costume. Chiseled jaw, a sinner's mouth, arrogantly slashed brows, and a perfect nose. In fact all of him was perfect. At least the parts that she could see. Gorgeous in a way that was hard to define. There was something different about him, a physical charisma or perhaps a foreign appeal? She couldn't put her finger on what it was that was so unique; she knew only that she'd never seen a more beautiful man, ever.

He wasn't beautiful in the "pretty" sense. He was beautiful in the rocky moors sense, or the Serengeti sense. Harsh and untamed. Awe-inspiring in a wholly intimidating way. And because she was intimidated, Stacey did what she excelled at.

She got spunky.

Cocking her hip to lean into the door edge, she flashed a bright smile. "Hi."

Bright, azure eyes widened, then narrowed.

"Who the hell are you?" the man demanded, his voice rumbling with a burr that was charming and delicious, even though his attitude wasn't.

"Nice to meet you, too."

"You're not Lyssa Bates," he rumbled.

"Damn. What gave me away? The short hair? The big butt?" She snapped her fingers. "I got it! I'm not drop-dead gorgeous and built like a brickhouse."

The corner of his luscious mouth twitched. He tried to hide it, but she saw it. "Honey, you're gorgeous and built, but you're not Lyssa Bates."

Stacey touched her nose, knowing that she had to be looking like Rudolph the Red-Nosed Reindeer and sporting bloodshot eyes to boot. Some women looked great when they cried. She wasn't one of them. And built? Ha! She'd had a kid. Nothing was where it used to be and she'd never dropped the last ten pounds from her pregnancy. Unable to think of a witty comeback because her brain was fried by his maybe-a-compliment, maybe-a-joke, she said, "Lyssa's out of town. I'm watching things for her while she's gone."

"Is Cross here?" He looked easily over her head and into the condo.

"Who?"

He looked back down at her, frowning. "Aidan Cross. He lives here."

"Uh, yeah. But if you think he'd let Lyssa go anywhere without him, you're nuts."

"True." Something passed through his eyes as he looked at her.

Jeez, she had to go on vacation to wherever the hell Aidan was from. Obviously Hunkalicious on the porch was from there, too. Same brogue. Same sword fetish. Same hotness level.

"I'm going to stay here until they get back," he pronounced, taking a step forward.

Stacey didn't budge. "No way."

He crossed his arms. "Listen, sweetheart, I'm not in the mood to play games. I feel like shit. I need to crash for a while."

"Listen, babe," she retorted, mimicking his pose. "I'm not playing. Sorry you feel like crap, but my day sucks, too. Go crash somewhere else."

She watched his jaw tighten. "Aidan wouldn't want me staying anywhere else."

"Oh yeah? He didn't say anything to me about anyone coming by. I don't know you from Adam."

"Connor Bruce." He thrust a massive hand at her. She

hesitated a moment, then took it. The heat of his palm burned her skin and spread tingles up her arm. She blinked.

"Stacey Daniels."

"Hi, Stacey." He tugged her into his chest, lifted her feet from the tile, and stepped into the condo, kicking the door shut behind them.

"Hey!" she protested, trying to ignore how delicious he smelled. Musky and exotic. Male. Sexual male. Dominant male. It made her want to bury her face in his powerful neck and breathe him in. Wrap her legs around his hips and rub up against him. Absolutely bizarre considering how pissed off at him she was.

"It stinks outside," he complained. "I'm not standing out there anymore."

"You can't just barge in here!"

"Sure, I can."

"Okay, you *can*. That doesn't mean you should."

Connor paused in the living room and looked around. Then he set her down, lifted his sword-holder-thingy over his head, and leaned it against the wall near the door.

"I'm going to bed." He stretched his arms and back in a pose that made her mouth water.

"It's still morning!"

"So? Don't touch that." He pointed to his sword, then turned toward the stairs.

"Fuck you." Stacey set her hands on her hips and glared.

He paused with one booted foot on the lower step. His gaze dropped to her bare feet, then rose slowly and hotly all the way back up, stopping at the juncture between her legs, then her breasts, before lingering over her lips and meeting her eyes. She'd never been stripped bare like that before in her life. She swore he'd looked right through her low-slung jeans and tank top to the skin below. Her breasts swelled, her nipples hardened. Without a bra—hey, she wasn't expecting company—it was obvious his perusal had turned her on.

"I'm tempted, darling." His brogue was thick and warm. "But I'm in no condition to do you justice right now. Ask me again when I wake up."

Her foot tapped on the carpet. "I'm not your honey, sweetheart, or darling. And if you go upstairs, I'm calling the police."

Connor grinned, which transformed his features from too-hot-to-handle to absolutely divine. "Sure thing. Make sure they bring handcuffs . . . and leave them behind."

"They won't be leaving *you* behind!" How in hell could the man make her hot and bothered *and* hot under the collar at the same time?

"Call Aidan," he suggested, climbing the stairs. "Or Lyssa. Tell them Connor's here. See ya later."

Running over to the stairs, Stacey prepared to yell up at him. Instead she found herself admiring his perfect ass. Her mouth snapped shut. She hustled to the kitchen and picked up the phone. A minute later, the odd phone-ring-ing-in-a-bucket sound told her the call was connecting to the hotel in Rosarito Beach, Mexico.

"Hello?"

"Hey, Doc." Climbing on to one of the barstools, Stacey snatched a pen out of the pen holder and began to doodle on the drawing pad by the cordless phone's base. She had to flip past several flawless renderings of Aidan in order to find a blank page. Most doctors had the worst handwriting. Lyssa was a veterinarian, but she had an amazing talent for drawing.

"Hey, Stace," Lyssa greeted, sounding relieved.

Stacey still hadn't figured out what it was that had Lyssa so stressed out. After years of looking run down and emotionally bereft, Lyssa had blossomed after reuniting with Aidan. She'd put on much needed weight and seemed more rested. But she also seemed anxious in a way that concerned Stacey no small amount. She worried that it might have something to do with Aidan. Maybe the fear that he wouldn't stick around? After all, the man had left Lyssa at some point and then come back for her.

"Are you okay, Doc?"

"Yes. Great. It's beautiful here."

Hearing the wary tone fade into dreamy, Stacey set aside her concern for her friend and returned her thoughts to her own dilemma. "Awesome. Hey, I've got a problem. Do you know a guy named Connor?"

"Connor?"

"Yeah, Connor. Big, blond, bad attitude?"

"Oh my god. . . .How do you know what he looks like?"

Stacey sighed. "So you do know him. I don't know if I'm relieved or bummed."

"Stacey. How do you know what Connor looks like?" Lyssa's voice now sounded the way it did when she had to explain a terminal illness to a patient's owner.

"He's here, Doc. Showed up about ten minutes ago and made himself at home. I told him to find another place to shack up, but—"

"No! Don't let him out of your sight!"

Jerking back from the handset, Stacey scowled down at the receiver, listening to the conversation from a safe distance since Lyssa was now shouting excitedly.

"He's Aidan's best friend . . . might get lost . . . don't let him leave . . . Stacey, are you there?"

"Yeah, I'm here," she replied, lifting the phone back up to her ear with a harsh exhale. "You know, the guy is hot as hell, but he's a real pain in the ass. Bossy and arrogant. Rude. JB is tough enough to live with, but two jerks at once?"

"I'll give you a raise," Lyssa cajoled.

"Right. I'm making more money than you now, I think." Not really, but they both knew she was overpaid. Lyssa was way too generous. "Seriously, I can handle him." *I want to handle him, all over.* That was part of the problem. She was always attracted to the wrong sort of guys. Always had been.

"Don't take it personally. They're all kind of . . . *abrupt* where Aidan comes from," Lyssa said.

"Which is where exactly?" Stacey had been trying to pin down a location for months.

"Somewhere by Scotland, I think."

"You still haven't asked him?"

"It's not important," Lyssa dismissed. "Aidan ran up to the liquor store for a six-pack, but when he gets back, he'll call and talk to Connor. I'll ask him to speak to him about proper politeness, okay?"

"Yeah, I can see that working." Stacey shook her head. "Connor's taking a nap now. Said he felt like shit or something. He showed up in some getup with a sword, looks like he came from a Star Wars convention or something."

"Oh. Crap." There was a long pause. "He's going to be sick for a bit, Stacey. Not long, several hours or overnight. He'll run a fever, get the chills."

"Huh? How do you know?" Lyssa was good, but come on. No doctor could diagnose a patient she hadn't seen or talked to.

"It's some freaky acclimation thing when they get off the plane. You know . . . new world and all that."

"New world?"

Lyssa cursed under her breath. "As in the-pilgrims-and-conquistador-type New World, not new world as in distant planets."

"Sure, Doc." Stacey tapped the pen against the tile countertop. "Whatever you say. Drink bottled water in Mexico, okay? I think they have nasty stuff in the taps down there."

Laughing, Lyssa said, "No worries. I'm not stoned."

"Uh huh. So, do you have a suggestion for the flu-like thing?"

"Tylenol, if he needs it. Otherwise, just let him sleep until he gets up on his own."

"That's easy enough."

"Great. Thank you for being so understanding about this. You're the best."

Stacey said good-bye with a promise to keep the handset nearby in anticipation of Aidan's phone call. Then she sat there for long moments, thinking back over her day, lingering over the moment she'd opened the front door and found Connor standing there. At least she wasn't concentrating so heavily on Justin and Tommy, but she shouldn't be thinking so hard about Connor either. She was hard up, that's all. She was not reverting to her tried-and-true pattern of being sexually attracted to a bad boy who would totally screw up her life.

Pushing off the stool, Stacey moved to the nearby dining table where her textbooks were spread out. She had finally gone back to college. The first time, she'd planned to be a writer and had been taking English and creative writing courses. Now, thirteen years later, she was fulfilling the requirements to become a veterinary technician.

She was content with that decision and proud of herself for going back to school. Dreams had to grow up just like people did. Raising a child alone had changed the nexus of her life.

That's where her focus should be. Not on the hunk in bed upstairs.

Easier said than done, of course.

The lushly curved redhead crossing the street wasn't human.

If Aidan Cross hadn't spent centuries killing Nightmares he might not have been observant enough to notice, and if he hadn't been deeply in love, he might have been more interested in the woman's body than her boots. But he *was* observant and firmly on the shelf, so while it was her crimson hair that caught his eye—and the eye of every other man walking the street—it was her combat boots that held his attention. They were black, self-sealing, and made of a material that didn't exist on Earth.

Aidan slowed his pace and adjusted his sunglasses to better shield his appearance. She was traversing the busy street at an angle, moving from the opposite sidewalk to the one he was walking on. He fell back, allowing more pedestrians to fill the space between them.

It was a gorgeous day in Rosarito Beach, Mexico. The sky was a pristine blue and dotted with pure white cottony clouds. Just beyond the shops to his left, the ocean kissed the shore in steady, rhythmic waves. The air was crisp and salty, the temperature warm, the breeze cool. The six-pack of Coronas he held in his hand were sweaty with condensation, and in the hotel room around the corner, his lover awaited him. Naked. Beautiful.

In danger.

He watched the Guardian—possibly an Elder—as she joined the light flow of foot traffic just a few feet ahead of him. Dressed in a short summer dress with thin straps and a flowered pattern on white, she might have looked innocent if not for the multiple tribal tattoos on her arms and the spiked leather bracelets.

Aidan rolled his shoulders back, limbering his body in preparation for battle. If the woman turned the upcoming corner and headed toward his hotel, he was ready to throw down.

Luckily for both of them, she didn't.

His relief was minimal. Every bit of his training told him to follow her and see what she was after. His heart, however, urged him to head down the small side street to his room and keep Lyssa safe. The struggle within him was worse than the one he'd been gearing up for. He *hated* sparring with women, detested it, but that would be easier to deal with than risking Lyssa's life.

Aidan began to cross the street that led to his hotel. He glanced to the side swiftly, scoping out the exterior of the building. Seeing nothing amiss, he clenched his jaw and kept going. He followed his quarry, ignoring the cramp in his gut that protested his decision. He couldn't go to Lyssa straightaway, regardless. It took him an average of thirty minutes to make the five-minute trip to the liquor store because of the precautions he took to make certain he wasn't followed.

Because of his anxiety, he was grateful that it wasn't long before the redhead deviated from the main street and made her way to a small dive motel that had definitely seen better days.

He fell farther behind.

When she tossed a furtive glance over her shoulder, Aidan linked arms with a nearby petite brunette and offered her a beer. His unsuspecting accomplice's surprise turned into sensual appreciation when she noted his appearance. He smiled down at her but kept his eye on the Guardian, who apparently found him innocuous enough to disregard.

"Thank you," he murmured to his companion when the redhead slipped into a room on the ground floor. Aidan noted the number on the door, then extricated himself carefully from the brunette. "Enjoy the beer."

She called after him, but he was already heading back the way he'd come. Back to Lyssa. He took a long, roundabout, and thoroughly unplanned route on the return trip to his hotel, pausing to examine various ponchos, hats, jewelry, and shot glasses displayed on tables near the street. He was acutely conscious of those who moved around and behind him. Only when he was absolutely certain he wasn't being followed, did he walk through the small open iron gate that decoratively bisected the manicured lawn of the hotel from the dusty public road.

As he stepped into their third floor room and engaged all the many locks on the door, Lyssa complained, "That took forever."

Aidan tossed his shades on the dresser by the television, set the remaining six-pack on the nightstand, and crawled over her sheet-draped body. Straddling her, he lowered his head and took her mouth, his eyes squeezing closed as relief flooded him. The vibrating anxiousness he'd felt over her safety faded when her slender arms wrapped around his neck and held him close. Her soft moan of welcome was music to his ears.

Tilting his head to better fit his mouth to hers, Aidan licked deep, his tongue sliding along hers, his senses inundated with the feel, smell, and taste of her. He growled deep in his throat as she arched upward, pressing her breasts into his chest.

"Umm. . ." she purred.

"Umm. . ." he agreed, lifting his head to nuzzle his nose against hers. Lowering to her side, he tucked her against him.

"You're not going to believe what I have to tell you," she murmured.

Her skin smelled like apples and her long blonde hair was damp from a recent shower. The sheets carried the lingering essence of them together, bare skin to bare skin, and a night of passion that had taken them from sunset to sunrise.

"Oh yeah?" He cupped the back of her head and kept her close.

"Yeah. Connor is at my house."

There was a long pause. "Imagine that."

Lyssa lifted her head and stared down at him. "Why don't you sound very surprised?"

Aidan exhaled harshly. "I saw another Guardian. She's staying in a hotel not too far from here."

"Oh shit."

He nodded wearily. "Exactly."

Chapter 4

Gasping for air and wracked by violent shivers, Connor emerged from the frigid lake and crawled up the sandy bank. As he pushed to his feet, his Elite uniform clung heavily to his body. He was so focused on fighting off the tension that came from hypothermia that he didn't realize he wasn't alone until he was tackled and knocked backward.

As a smaller, wirier body wrapped around his, his roar of outrage reflected off the surface of the water and released his mounting tension. Connor twisted and grappled with his assailant until the moment they both fell back into the lake in an explosion of water and slapping skin.

The sting of the unexpected impact combined with the shock of being attacked really, really pissed Connor off. He grabbed his assailant by the scruff of his robes and dragged him onto the shore.

"Wait!" Dressed in gray, the man could only be an Elder.

Unfortunately for him, Connor wasn't feeling so charitable toward Elders right now and he was in the mood to kick some serious ass. He reached over his shoulder and pulled his glaive free of its scabbard. "If you had a death wish, old man," he growled, "you should have just said so outright."

"Cross needs you."

Connor stiffened at the sound of the familiar voice. Of course it couldn't be just any Elder. Not on a crappy day such as today. It had to be Elder Sheron. His instructor from the Elite Academy.

"What Cross needs are answers, Sheron. We all need answers."

The Elder pushed back the soaked cowl that hid his face and Connor took a good look at the man who had helped to mold him into the warrior he was today. Sheron's appearance had changed so drastically he was nearly unrecognizable as the vigorous Master he had once been. His dark brown hair was now pure white, the suntanned skin now an unhealthy pale, and his pupils were so wide and dark they swallowed the whites of his eyes all together. In that respect he looked very much like the thing that had been sealed up in the Temple.

Disgust filled Connor only to be quickly replaced by fury. Aidan had looked up to Sheron as one would a father. Deserted by his birth parents for entering the Elite Academy, Aidan had needed a parental figure and turned to Sheron to fill that role. It angered Conner further to think that his friend's trust had been so misplaced.

For his part, Connor came from a long line of Elite Warriors. Male and female alike, the Bruces all joined the Elite. Live and die by the sword *was their family creed, which was why Connor* had little patience for lies and deceit. Time was precious, even for a nearly immortal.

Aidan's parents, however, were a different breed of Guardian altogether—one a Healing Guardian, the other a Nurturer. They couldn't understand the path their son had chosen and the constant questions they'd pestered Aidan with had eventually driven him away. The Crosses couldn't understand why their only child needed to be working against the Nightmares, not repairing the damage they caused after the fact. Since they were the only family Aidan had, that left him with only two bonds—Connor and Sheron.

And Sheron had been unworthy of such esteem and affection.

"Others have been sent to the mortal plane after Cross," Sheron said grimly, both hands clasped tightly around the hilt of his sword. "Powerful Elders. He will require assistance."

"We're not as out of the loop as you might think," Connor scoffed, circling his adversary with slow, steady steps. "And while you're in a sharing mood, why don't you explain what that thing was in the Temple?"

Sheron stilled, his sword lowered. "I warned them. I told them the system was untried and unsecured. It was too risky, but they were determined."

"What are you talking about?" Connor's gaze narrowed on the Elder, his wariness increasing. He'd seen this ruse before, the one where a combatant pretended to lose interest in the fight only to strike with the element of surprise.

Sheron paused mid-step. "The cavern was our primary means of controlling the flow between the mortal plane and the Twilight, but we knew that such heavy reliance on one location left us too vulnerable. We altered a room in the Temple of the Elders in an effort to attract Medium slipstreams. It worked, to a lesser extent. But the Temple is not secure from Nightmares."

"It isn't?" That struck a deep cord of unease in Connor. He had always looked at the shining white edifice of the Temple and felt peace. It was untainted by their enemy and filled with the history of his people in the Hall of Knowledge. While he'd never personally made use of the information there, it had calmed him to think of it.

"No." Sheron pushed back the sodden shank of pure white hair that fell over his brow. "The Nightmares have grown more desperate. The older ones have learned to stalk their prey, rather than simply attack in a frenzy. Every shadow you see is suspect and only the cavern is safe, though we are not certain why. Something to do with the water, I suspect."

"Maybe it's too damn cold," Connor suggested, shivering in the gentle breeze. With a wave of his hand, he heated the air around him, forming an insulating pocket. Outside of that immediate space, the velocity of the breeze picked up exponentially and the sky darkened with roiling clouds.

"We do not know, Bruce. I tried to dissuade the others, but they felt the risk was worth the gain."

"And what exactly is the risk?"

Sheron's lips pursed. "That Nightmares will. . ."

Thunder cracked and blackness descended in an all-consuming blanket. The Elder screamed and the clouds began to take shape, reconstituting into the familiar form of Nightmares.

Thousands of them. . .

Connor awoke in terror.

He jackknifed upward in the bed, startled by his surroundings, his brain taking a moment too long to register where he was. His heart raced, his skin was coated in sweat.

The mortal plane. He was in hell.

His chest heaved with labored breaths as he swung his legs off the side of the bed and dropped his head into his hands.

Nightmares, the bastards.

As if the smells of this world weren't bad enough, now he had Nightmares to deal with.

Disgusted, Connor pushed heavily to his feet and stripped out of his clothes, leaving them in a pile on the floor. He opened the door to the guest room he'd selected after seeing that the other two bedrooms were occupied. One was the master suite, the other smelled like the hottie who had opened the front door to him.

His mouth curved grimly. At least there was something—*someone*—he liked about this place.

Stacey was round, ripe, curvy perfection with those full hips, shapely ass, and big tits. She was the kind of woman a man could hang on to and ride hard.

His dick swelled at the thought and he moaned softly, his blood beginning to simmer from the combination of too long abstaining, too shitty a day, and too fine a woman. He wanted to wrap his fist into that riot of tight black corkscrew curls and possess that lush red mouth of hers. Even with teary green eyes and red nose, her heart-shaped face had been alluring in the basest sense. He wanted to see it flushed, glistening with sweat, and etched with the tormented need for orgasm. If he hadn't felt as if he was dying, he would have cheered her up right.

Of course, better late than never. He needed cheering up, too. He felt torn—angry and disillusioned and lost. It was the last that affected him most. He prized a firm foundation. Aidan was the adventurer. Connor liked his life well-defined and without surprises. He didn't like this sensation of free-falling and knew just how to find a spot of peace in a frenetic world.

That spot was inside Stacey.

And she was downstairs waiting for him. Although she didn't know it yet.

Connor went into the guest bathroom and took a cold shower. It felt like heaven to wash up after the day he'd had so far and when he stepped out into the hallway a few minutes later, he felt better contained. Less restless and more in control.

He thought about getting dressed before heading downstairs in search of food, then decided against it. He didn't feel like putting his uniform back on until it was cleaned and as far as he was concerned, the towel wrapped around his hips made him decent. His lack of attire might just rile Stacey, too, which could be the impetus needed to get her into his bed. Passion of any kind could be turned to passion of the sexual kind, with the right persuasion. And Stacey already wanted him—those long, tight nipples proved it—even if she didn't *want* to want him.

He'd fulfilled enough human fantasies to know that sometimes women denied their desires for reasons that had nothing to do with the sex itself. Whether a man had a good job, liked kids, was faithful, a decent cook, knew how to fix cars, or wore a suit to work—the reasons for saying "no" to sex were way more numerous than the reasons for saying "yes."

Guardians didn't have such unrelated concerns. Sex was comfort and desire and a necessary slaking of needs. It promoted health and elevated moods. It was as necessary as breathing, and although some Guardians partnered permanently, most kept their options open.

He needed comfort now and forgetfulness, and if he gave Stacey more reasons to say "yes" than he did to say "no," he could have her. And he wanted her. Badly.

As Connor stepped off the last stair onto the marble

tile of the foyer, he shot a quick glance at the decorative window above the sliding glass patio door. The reddish tint to the sunlight told him it was late afternoon, and a glance at the cable box above the television affirmed that it was a little past six o'clock.

"I'm not trying to guilt-trip you!" Stacey protested hotly.

Who the hell was visiting?

He was about to return to his room for his pants when she said, "I can't help it if I sound sad. I miss you. What kind of mother would I be if I didn't miss you? That doesn't mean I'm trying to make you feel bad for going!"

She was on the phone. He felt the tension in his shoulders fade. They were alone after all. Just what he needed. He didn't think he could handle a larger interaction at this point. His nerves were stretched too thin.

Connor crossed the living room and paused on the threshold of the dining room. Stacey was facing away from him, her back tense, her hand rubbing at the back of her neck.

Damn, she had a nice ass. Big, she'd called it. He had to admit it wasn't small, but it was tight and round and more than a handful. He wanted to palm those firm cheeks while he tilted her hips to the perfect angle to take his cock to the root. Hard and deep fucking . . . He wanted it like he wanted to breathe, wanted the tangible connection to another person. A shudder of longing wracked the length of his frame. Then her voice grew more agitated and he frowned.

"I understand you haven't seen him in years. As if I could forget that . . . No, that wasn't a dig . . . Jesus, it's the goddamned truth . . . he hasn't sent me a dime of support for you! I'm not making it up . . . *Get over it?* He's skiing and I'm broke, and *I'm* supposed to get over it? Justin? *Justin?* Honey . . .?" She sighed heavily and slammed the phone back into its cradle. "Shit!"

Connor watched as she ran both of her hands through her riotous curls. Then he noted that her shoulders were shaking with silent sobs. Suddenly, the need to fuck and forget became something else entirely. The need to share misery, to sympathize.

"Hey," he rumbled softly, relating to the frustration and grief he heard in her curse.

She screeched and leaped at least a foot or more into the air.

"Fuckin' A!" she yelled, turning to glare at him with a hand pressed over her heart. Tears hung on thick black lashes and stained her pale cheeks. "You scared me to death!"

"I'm sorry."

Her gaze dropped to his hips and the boner that tented his towel, parting the two halves to reveal his thigh all the way to his waist. "Oh my god."

His lust, her pain, and the Nightmares of just moments ago made false charm impossible. "You have the loveliest ass I've ever seen," he explained.

"I have a lovely . . .?" She blinked but didn't look away. "You're walking around the house half-naked with a hard-on and all you can say is 'you have a lovely ass?'"

"I can be fully naked, if you prefer."

"Oh, hell no." Her arms crossed over her chest, which only served to accentuate her braless breasts. Desire, building for weeks, flared across his skin and left a light mist of sweat behind. "The house doesn't come with those kind of benefits."

"I don't care what the house comes with," he said honestly. She was soft, warm, emotional woman. That's what he needed. "I want to know what *you* come with. A soft touch? Something rougher? Do you like to be loved fast and hard? Or long and slow? What makes you hoarse, sweetheart?"

"Jesus! Don't beat around the bush or anything."

Connor watched her pupils dilate, an unconscious invitation. He stepped closer. Carefully. No quick movements, because he could tell she was in the grip of the fight-or-flight response and he didn't want her to run. Doubted he could let her run.

"I've no patience for lies at the moment," he murmured. "I want you. A night with you would be heaven after what I've gone through recently. I don't like it here. I'm homesick and just plain sick."

"S-sorry—" Stacey swallowed hard, her eyes big in her piquant face, her tongue darting out to wet cherry red lips. "Sorry to disappoint you, but I can't tonight. I have a headache."

He stepped closer.

She backed up and bumped into a barstool. Her chest lifted and fell rapidly, as did his. Her nostrils flared, sensing danger. Inside him, coiled tightly, was the need to snatch her close. To convince her to stay and say yes. To prevent her from denying that she was his, which some primitive voice inside him was whispering she was. *Mine,* it insisted. *She's mine.*

Something inside *her* understood.

"We're both having a crappy day," he managed, his voice raspier than he would have liked. "Why should we have a crappy night, too?"

"Sex won't fix my problem."

As she wrapped her hands around the edge of the wooden stool seat, her chin lifted. The pose thrust her breasts forward wantonly, defiantly, stirring the need he felt into raging hunger. A rough growl filled the space between them and she gasped softly. Her nipples beaded up tight, pushing against the loose cotton ribbing of her tank top.

Connor's cock swelled further, a response he was unable to hide as scantily dressed as he was. He wanted her. *Now.* Wanted to forget that he wasn't at home, that he might never go home. Wanted to forget that he'd been lied to and deceived. Wanted to wrap himself around a warm, willing woman and help her forget her pain, too. It was what he did, what he knew, what he excelled at. What grounded him. And this time it would be for real. Not a dream or a fantasy.

He could sense the vibrating anxiety in her, the tinge of desperation, the need to scream out her frustration and anger and hurt. The need to connect to someone who had absolutely nothing to do with anything. Someone blameless, without baggage or expectation, a guilt-free pleasure. She just needed a little push.

Tugging at his towel, Connor let it drop to the floor.

"Good grief," she muttered. "You're incredible."

With a gentle smile, he deliberately took her statement in a way it wasn't intended. "Ah, but I haven't even started yet."

* * *

The low, deep brogue wrapped around Stacey's spine, then slid down in a heated glide.

Infuriated with herself for being aroused, she stared at the tall, golden, gorgeous—impossibly gorgeous—*naked* man striding toward her. Unable to look away from the beautifully honed muscles drenched in tawny skin. Or the dark honey hair that hung over a strong brow. Or the Caribbean blue eyes that roamed her body from head to toe, the gaze hot and lustful but tender, too.

His sinfully sensual mouth was framed by lines of tension and stress, a sight that tempted her to kiss his troubles away. Whatever they might be.

As if it that was possible. Connor Bruce seemed to be an island unto himself. There was something inherently dangerous about him, something savage and untamed. He seemed . . . *dark* somehow, tormented. A feeling she understood because she presently felt that way herself. Barely leashed. Tense. She wanted to drive up to Big Bear and tell Justin and Tommy both that one fucking ski trip did not make Tommy Father of the Century.

Frustrated with her inability to "get over it," Stacey imprudently ogled Connor's luscious cock instead. After all, he was waving it around . . .

"It's all yours," he purred, coming at her with a devastating combination of determination and mouth-watering, finely honed abs. She looked up and saw challenge within the depths of his blue eyes. He knew she couldn't help but look and covet what he offered so bluntly. "And you're all mine."

God, how she wished she could laugh that off. Considering how long they'd known each other, that comment should have been funny as hell. But Connor was too primitive a male to dismiss when he became possessive. Just as she, apparently, was primitive enough to enjoy being dragged back to his cave by her hair.

There was something *very* wrong with a man being that perfect. Six feet plus of pure, potent male. He was big, broad, and bad. Irresistibly bad. And unapologetic about it. She might have been able to resist if that were all he was. But he seemed vulnerable, too, in a way she couldn't define. It called to her, though, whatever it was. Deeply. She found herself wanting to soothe him, embrace him, make him smile.

Her gaze once again fell helplessly to the long, thick cock that led the way for him. That was perfect, too. She couldn't find a damn thing wrong with his body and she was trying. Boy, was she trying. He was savagely beautiful and forbiddingly sexy, but she wasn't giving in. No way. She was drooling over him, yes, but she was not going to repeat her past mistakes. She didn't even know the guy, for chrissakes!

"Does that Conan the Barbarian act work for you?" she asked with an arched brow, acting for all she was worth. "'Cuz it sure as hell isn't working for me."

His lips curved in a boyish smile. She was stunned by her reaction to it. It was the kind of charming curve that made one want to smile back.

"Prove it." His long, easy stride made her shiver. She gripped the seat behind her with such force she broke a nail and a small sound of dismay escaped her. It gave away too much, that soft breathy cry. She could tell it did, because his gaze heated and darkened, and his cock swelled even further. Her mouth dried at the sight.

Lord have mercy. The thick length was lined with throbbing veins that forced her to bite back a moan of longing. Porn stars would pay for that cock. Shit, women paid for cocks such as his, molded in plastic with a speed control switch.

"Are you double-dog daring me?" she muttered, her gaze riveted by the sheer predatory grace of his movements. She wondered how he moved while fucking and the thought made her damp between the legs.

She was lonely, tired, frustrated by the hand life had dealt her, and pissed off enough to want to shed her unappreciated-mommy role for an hour or two. *Get over it?* Sure. What better way to get over it than to get under a man like Connor Bruce?

"Let me hold you," he murmured, his accent a gentle enticement.

Stacey didn't move. She couldn't.

As he came closer, she held her breath, knowing that her resistance to his very attractive but impractical offer would weaken if she smelled him. The scent of his skin was unique. A bit spicy, a bit musky. One hundred percent male. Pure Connor. Inhaling would sharpen the images already in her mind of him suspended above her, his arms bulging as he held his weight aloft, his abdominal muscles lacing tight as he pumped his thick cock in and out of her, his gorgeous features taut with lust.

The way he looked right now.

Panicked at her craving, Stacey shook her head violently

and jumped quickly to the side, hoping to skirt the dining table and . . . hoping he'd chase her.

Which he did.

Connor lunged and caught her easily, his steely arm banding around her waist and hauling her back against him. The confinement awakened the full force of her desire, making her soften and grow slick with anticipation.

"Let me, Stacey." The tone of his voice changed, became urgent and thick with need. "I need you. You need me. Let it happen."

The fierceness of his desire was evident in every line of his big body. It was tangible and very, very tempting.

It was also insane.

"Damn it!" she snapped, struggling because it turned her on more to do so, not because she had any expectation of getting away. "You can't just haul me off to bed!"

"You're right. I won't make it that far. Right here will have to do."

"Here?" she croaked. "This is nuts! We don't even know each other!"

He tightened his embrace and nuzzled against her sweetly, his tongue gliding across the fluttering pulse at her throat. It made her dizzy to be held by him, surrounded by his scent and his attention to detail. She had no doubt that Connor would find every erogenous zone on her body. She also had no doubt that she wanted him to. God, it had been so long since she'd had great sex with someone who was focused on pleasuring her. Someone who seemed to *need* to pleasure her.

"You're thinking too much," he whispered with his

lips to her ear. He reached up and cupped her unfettered breast. His palm was warm, his squeeze firm but gentle. His thumb and forefinger pinched her nipple, rolled it, tugged it. She writhed as the sensation shot straight to her sex and tingled madly. A rough sound rumbled up from his chest.

The urge to close her eyes and melt into him was strong. "People don't just hop into bed with strangers because they had a shitty day."

"Why not? Why deny yourself something you want?"

"It's called maturity." She changed tactics and hung like a deadweight in his arms. He didn't appear to notice. The man was brawny enough to carry an elephant.

"Sounds like self-torture to me."

"I suppose you just barrel through life thinking you can do whatever you damn well please because you're hot."

He pressed a hard, quick kiss to her temple and used both hands to knead her breasts. "You're hot and you don't do what you want."

Stacey snorted. "Compliments will not get you into my pants."

Connor reached up and cupped her cheek, angling her mouth to meet his. "No," he whispered against her lips, "but this will."

He yanked open her button fly, then shoved his hand into her jeans.

"No . . ."

His tongue thrust deep into her mouth, stemming her protest. He cupped her through her lace thong. "Yes," he purred, rubbing her swollen, needy pussy with skillful fingers, "you're wet, sweetheart."

She whimpered as he pushed the intruding material out of the way and touched her skin-to-skin.

"Tell me you want me," he rasped, the callused tip of his index finger sliding between her folds and stroking over her engorged clit. Back and forth. Caressing, circling.

The tension was intense, her breath panting, her legs straining.

"Oh! I'm going to come . . . Oh god . . ." Jesus, she'd gone so long without she was hair-trigger ready.

"Tell me you want me," he repeated.

Her hips swiveled and rocked into that maddening finger. "Does it matter?" she gasped, bucking like a wild thing within the cage of his powerful arms.

"Yes." His teeth sank into the taut muscle at her neck and she cried out in surprise. "It does. I want you. I want you to want me back."

Two long, thick fingers were pushing into her and she spasmed on the verge of climax. Her eyes closed and her head fell back against his chest. She was shivering violently, overwhelmed, teary. Her entire day had been an emotional overload and now he'd added lust and desire to the mix.

"Yes . . ." she sobbed, her nails digging into the forearm crossing between her breasts. It felt so good to be held and embraced. Wanted.

"Push your jeans down."

Stacey grabbed her waistband and shimmied her pants down to her knees, blinking back hot tears. Straightening, she reached for her purse on the granite-topped breakfast bar and pulled out the string of condoms she'd picked up a week ago. They were Magnum XL, a joke she thought would add levity to her upcoming "birds and the bees" talk. Now, she hoped they weren't too small. Connor was hung, a circumstance that only made her wetter, less resistant. My god . . . he was going to be *in* her . . . *soon* . . .

He thrust one foot between her legs and stepped down, shoving her pants down to the floor. Her butt bumped against his steely erection and his breath hissed between his teeth. His grip on her torso tightened. Her heart leapt with a flare of fright. He was a huge man and he seemed barely in control.

"Shh," he crooned, releasing her only long enough to put his hand beneath her shirt. With his hand over her racing heart, he paused, his chest heaving against her back. His face was damp and feverishly hot, and he pressed his cheek to hers roughly. "This isn't me. I'm not like this. I'm pushing you too fast—"

"I'm not like this either," she whispered, setting her hand over his through her tank top and moving it down to her breast. Her fingers rested atop his and squeezed, urging him to fondle the heavy, aching weight of her flesh. "And you're not going fast enough."

"I'm going to fuck you. I can't help it." His brogue was so thick she could hardly understand him. "Hard and fast. Then we'll start over. I'll make it good for you. Do it right."

Shaking her head, Stacey leaned forward, offering the most private part of her body to him. "Just do it. Right or wrong."

Connor rumbled something, then he tore open the box of condoms and broke into a foil packet. She forced herself to breathe in and out carefully, willing her brain to feel less dizzy, telling herself that this was a one-night stand, not a goddamn relationship. He didn't have to be "permanent" material; he just had to carry the right equipment and show her some consideration.

The man was best friends with Aidan, who was a great guy. That didn't make Connor a great guy, but it did make him slightly better than a complete stranger. And they were adults. They could indulge in a little gratuitous sex and still be civil. She wasn't repeating past mistakes, because she had no expectations that this would go beyond an orgasm. Right? *Right?*

Stacey had almost convinced herself that this encounter was only slightly more involved that using a vibrator when Connor grasped her thighs and lifted her effortlessly, stealing her balance in more ways than one. With a startled cry, she clung to the barstool and felt the world tilt.

Then he was there, the fat tip of him notching into the slick, slitted entrance to her pussy. She moaned as he nudged and he made a soothing sound that might have calmed her if she weren't out of her mind with lust and a hundred other emotions.

"Relax," he urged hoarsely. "Let me in. I've got you."

Panting, she willed herself limp, afraid that she would be too heavy and startled to realize that he held her aloft easily. He eased in an inch and she felt every groove and vein of him because she hugged him so tightly.

"Oh!"

"Touch yourself." Connor shuddered as he fed more of his thick cock into her. "Get yourself off. You're so tight . . ."

Stacey clung to the seat with one arm, while reaching a hand between her legs to rub. She was stretched wide and tight to accommodate him, which exposed her clit even further from its hood. She was swollen, hot, slick; more aroused than she'd ever remembered being. He sank deeper, pushing with shallow, rapid digs that made her mewl and beg. Her pussy fluttered around his cock and he groaned, his fingertips digging into the flesh of her thighs.

"That's it, baby," he whispered hoarsely. "Suck me in. Take all of me."

With a relieved cry, she climaxed hard, her fingers rubbing, her cunt flooding with moisture, easing his way. He thrust hard and hilted with a grunt. In a distant part of her brain Stacey heard the phone ringing, but it didn't mean anything and a moment later all she could hear was the deafening rush of blood in her ears.

"Hang on," he ordered. He began to pound her pussy in a savage rhythm, pumping high and hard, his powerful thighs flexing between hers. Her eyes closed and her cheek rested against the hard wooden seat, sliding back and forth in her own sweat, her body on fire because his was. His cock was like a burning brand inside her. She was hot, but he was hotter.

Unbelievably, the tension coiled tight again, building . . . growing. . . .His heavy balls smacked repeatedly against her tender clit, the sound so erotic she shivered with renewed arousal. The rim of his cockhead grazed a tender spot inside her and she was instantly on the edge.

"Oh god," she whimpered, "I'm coming again."

He spread her legs wide and struck deep, expertly stroking across that magic place inside her that caused her to wail in mindless pleasure. His satisfaction was tangible as she arched taut beneath his relentless drives.

For all his warnings of haste, he seemed in no hurry to come now that he was in her. Unable to bear anymore and slightly afraid of what would happen to her if she climaxed that hard again, Stacey reached between her legs and touched his swinging balls.

Connor cursed and swelled, stuffing her full. "I'm not going to last . . ."

Tightening down, she hugged him with her inner muscles. He jerked violently and with a guttural shout began to come. His cock strained and bucked with the force of his ejaculations in a brutal, wrenching orgasm. He lowered, taking her with him. First to his knees, then to his back, his sweat soaking her tank. His brawny arms circled around her. All the way to the floor.

Where he held her with his lips to her temple, still coming . . .

# Chapter 5

"Hi! You've reached Dr. Lyssa Bates and Aidan Cross. We're sorry we're not available to answer your call right now. If this is an emergency . . ."

Aidan hung up the phone with a muttered curse and flopped back onto the bed.

Lyssa pushed up onto one elbow and stared down at him with her big dark eyes. "No answer?"

He shook his head.

"Maybe Connor is still sleeping and Stacey ran out for a bite," she suggested.

"Maybe. We'll have to try again later on the cell phone when we cross back over into San Ysidro."

He watched the pendant he had given her for protection swing gently between her full breasts. When they'd first met, she had been plagued by restless sleep, a result of her uncanny ability to block both Guardians and Nightmares from her dreams. Now she was a vision, her pale skin kissed by the sun, her eyes no longer marred by shadows, her lush figure filled out and not so lean. But as wonderful as the package was, it was the contents he loved—her kindness and compassion, her deep love for him, and her desire for his happiness.

"Are you sure it was a Guardian you saw earlier?" she asked for the hundredth time, her hand caressing the hard ripples of his naked abdomen.

"Pretty damn sure. Either that or an Elder. We'll know for certain when we head back over there and I search her room."

Lyssa's wince caused him to cup the back of her head and pull her down for a quick, hard kiss to her forehead.

"Trust me," he urged.

"I do. You know I do." She sighed, her thick lashes lowering to hide her thoughts. "That doesn't mean I'm not going to freak out when you put yourself in danger. The thought of you hurt terrifies me."

"I know how you feel, Hot Stuff, because I feel the same way about you. That's why we have to follow through. If we're being hunted, I have to know." Aidan lifted his hand and rubbed a lock of her hair between his fingertips. "We need to know if she's after you, or the *taza*. Or both. Shit, maybe she's here for something we don't know about yet."

Lyssa sat up and arranged herself against the headboard. She sighed, the sound blending with the waves that crashed on the beach outside their balcony. "Being the Key sucks."

He hummed a soothing sound. "I'm sorry, baby."

There was nothing more he could say and they both knew it.

"It's worth it to be with you." Her sweet voice was low and fervent.

He lifted her hand to his lips and kissed the knuckles. "Want one last beer before we check out?"

Her smile affected him deeply, tempting him to stay in bed longer when they really had to be going. Aidan sat up and left the bed before his heart overruled his brain, something it did often because he loved Lyssa so much. It drove him crazy that he couldn't shake the feeling that their time together was limited, that there was an hourglass somewhere draining the sands of time. For an immortal, that was saying something. And what it was saying wasn't good.

"You're always taking care of me," she murmured. "Looking after me, supporting me. I don't know what I'd do without you."

"You'll never find out, Hot Stuff."

Lyssa stared into the dark blue eyes of her lover and hated the anxiety that vibrated deep within her, the feeling of dread and doom that was making her nauseous. Her instinctual response to hearing that a Guardian was nearby was to run far away, not hunt them down and find out what they wanted.

She watched Aidan move to the table by the open sliding glass door. He used his pocket knife to slice up one of the dozen limes he'd picked up yesterday, then he cradled a handful of slices in his palms and carried them back to the nightstand.

Enamored with the sheer beauty of his body, Lyssa was riveted by the view of Aidan approaching in a delicious display of golden rippling abs and outstretched hands dripping lime juice. Well over six feet of pure, unadulter-ated, luscious male. The man of her dreams. Literally. A man who'd left everything behind to be with her. A man who was determined to save her from his own people who wanted her dead, regardless of any risk to himself. She loved him so much it burned like fire in her chest, making it hard to breath.

"Do you ever consider that protecting me, working for McDougal, and hunting the artifacts are altogether too much for you to handle by yourself?" She watched him sit on the edge of the mattress and reached out to rest her hand atop his shoulder. The muscles bunched as he popped the cap off the bottle and stuffed the opening with a lime slice. The scent of his skin, something exotic and spicy, hit her at the same moment as the smell of tangy citrus. "If there is one Guardian here, there could be more."

He twisted and met her gaze head on. His irises were an intense deep blue, resembling a rich sapphire. Unique, just as the rest of him was. Sculpted jaw and winged brows, raven-black hair, and a body built for a woman's pleasure. He was hard, chiseled, and dangerously gorgeous. And he was hers. She refused to lose him.

"I know." He passed the bottle to her, then reached for his own.

The powerful muscles in his arms flexed with the move-ment, inciting shivers of sensual awareness in her. They'd spent all day in bed, indulging in one another, yet she wanted him still. She would always hunger for him and the physical connection that made their love a tangible thing.

"Connor would only have come if it were a matter of life

or death," he said, sounding weary. "Unlike me, he was happy in the Twilight. To him this plane is probably hell."

"Great," she muttered. "Sounds promising."

Aidan had refuted the ancient prophecy of his people that said she was the Key destined to destroy his world and the human world. He had left his home in the Twilight because of his love for her. No other Guardian would have such a potent impetus.

"Don't give up hope yet." He joined her against the headboard, stretching out his long legs bared by loose khaki shorts. Dusk was rapidly turning into night, but neither of them made any effort to turn on a lamp. The bathroom door was cracked and the light spilling from there was enough for both of them.

Tipping the bottle up, Aidan drank in large gulps and then settled back with the beer in his lap. "Maybe there is a way to track the Guardians through dreams now that they're here. Maybe he brought good news."

"I hate feeling so helpless." Lyssa's fingers picked restlessly at the bottle label, her eyes drifting to the sword and scabbard lying atop a nearby chair. "I can't read your language, so I can't help you with deciphering the journals you stole."

"Borrowed indefinitely," he corrected, laughing.

She snorted. "I have no combat skills, so I can't help you fight. I don't have centuries of memories like you do, so I can't help you find the artifacts."

He reached out and stilled her restless fingers with an icy, wet hand. "That doesn't mean you're not helping. Your 'very important job' is to keep me recharged. That's why I brought you along this time."

"I wanted to come. I hate it when you're gone for days or weeks at a time. I miss you too much."

Aidan looked at her with a soft smile. "I need you with me. It's not merely a matter of convenience. Every time you take a breath, you give me reason to live. Every time you smile, you give me hope. Every time you touch me, you make my dreams come true. You keep me going, Hot Stuff."

"Aidan . . ." Her eyes stung. He could say the corniest shit, but it never sounded corny coming from him. He put one hundred percent of his effort into everything he did—even loving her.

"I was dying before I met you."

She knew he had been. Not physically, but emotionally. Weary of the stalemate in the war against the Nightmares and disheartened by his lack of connection to anyone, Aidan had been merely surviving. Not living. He'd shared with her how lonely he had been, but he didn't have to say it aloud. She had seen the emptiness in his eyes.

"I love you." She leaned over and pressed her lips to his.

Despite their differences—which were as vast as being from two separate species—they were very much alike. Tormented by lack of dreams, she'd been too exhausted for any kind of life beyond work. Aidan's love gave her optimism for the future.

"You damn well better," he teased, cupping the back of her head and keeping her close when she would have pulled back. He licked her lips and then nipped the lower one with his teeth. She moaned in invitation.

"I want to oblige you," he whispered, "but we're going to have to leave soon."

Lyssa nodded and caught her pendant in her fist. Odd how a stone made of Nightmare ash melted into a glass-like material from the decimated Guardian homeworld could change her life. But it radiated a unique energy—a combination of Guardian and Nightmare that kept both factions at bay in her dreams, enabling her to sleep normally. "I tossed my stuff in the duffel when I got out of the shower earlier."

"Perfect." He kissed the tip of her nose. "We should wait until it is completely dark to check out. Then I'm going to ransack that motel room and hopefully figure out what our Guardian friend is up to. We can take off from there and head down to Ensenada, where we'll pick up the relic for McDougal and meet with the shaman there."

"Got it. I'm the getaway driver."

"Yep, lead foot." Aidan took another long pull of his beer. "At least this time I was able to guarantee us two weeks' worth of search time. I'm not leaving Mexico without that *taza*."

Earlier in the month he had been only hours away from an auction bid on an obscure dream doll when his employer, Sean McDougal, called him back to California for his opinion on a possible sword purchase. Aidan had been furious but didn't have any choice in the matter.

McDougal was an eccentric and exceptionally wealthy collector of antiquities, and Aidan's first-hand knowledge of history and his expert grasp of every language on Earth had made him perfect for the job of McDougal's acquisitions team leader. The position provided him with the means to travel the world at will, all expenses paid, truly the only way they could afford to have Aidan searching for the artifacts mentioned in the Elders' journals. Keeping his job was a necessity.

"I don't understand why the Elders waited until now to send Guardians after the artifacts," Lyssa said, thinking aloud. "Why not before you came here?"

"Because before the Key—*you*—were found, they were safer here. The Twilight is small. Over centuries, the items would have been discovered there. Here, they were far from the reach of the curious."

Heaving out her breath, Lyssa tossed back the sheets and slid off the bed. Aidan's low whistle of appreciation as she stood made her smile. She grabbed a spaghetti-strapped sundress and slipped it over her head, then grabbed her beer and went out to the balcony to admire the last of the coastal sunset. A moment later, his arms bracketed her, one hand clutching the railing, the other holding his beer. His lips nuzzled the top of her shoulder and the embrace of his much larger body was a welcome comfort.

The scents of a barbeque drifted up from somewhere below. Nearby, on the small plastic table in the corner of the balcony, an open bottle of suntan oil released the faint smell of coconut. For Lyssa, the sights and smells inundating her were expected for a busy tourist resort town in Baja California. She worried about Aidan, though, knowing that centuries of living in a bubble—technically a conduit between two planes of existence, as he had explained—had made such a barrage of sensual input intense and disturbing.

"Do you miss it?" she asked softly. "The Twilight?"

She felt his smile curve against her skin. "Not in the way you might think."

Lyssa turned in his arms and faced him, finding joy in the mischievous gleam in his blue eyes. "Oh?"

"I miss the absolute quiet sometimes and the familiarity of my house, but only because I want to take you there. I want to be somewhere private with you, somewhere safe. Where time isn't a concern and I can turn off every noise. I want to hear nothing but you . . . the sounds you make when I'm inside you."

"That would be wonderful," she breathed, wrapping her arms around his lean waist, wrapping her love around his.

"It's my dream," he murmured, resting his chin on the top of her head. "Lucky for us, we know dreams come true."

Stacey stirred first. Connor fought the urge to hold her and keep her close. She was wiggling that lush ass against his loins and his cock responded admirably, especially considering he still felt less than his best. Traveling between planes of existence sure took a lot out of a guy.

"My God," she breathed. "How can you still have an erection after *that*?"

He buried a chuckle in the fragrant mass of black glossy curls and tightened his embrace. Just as he'd expected, she was soft and warm, a much appreciated refuge and delight in a world gone to shit. Never one to hide from trouble, he was nevertheless tempted to hide with Stacey. Just hole up in a bedroom somewhere and pretend that none of the last few weeks had ever happened. "You're rubbing and grinding your hot little body all over me. I would be worried if I *weren't* hard."

"You're insane. I'm wiped out."

"Are you?" he purred, sliding one hand between her spread legs. He arched his hips upwards, pushing his cock deeper into her while cupping a full breast with his free hand. With reverent fingertips he circled her clit, careful to move gently after her earlier frantic rubbing. "I'll do all the work, don't worry."

"I-I'm not . . . Oh! I can't . . ."

"Sure you can, darlin'." Connor licked around the shell of her ear, then dipped his tongue inside. She shivered and creamed around his cock. It felt delicious and he nudged his hips upward in gentle pushes, massaging inside her delectably tight cunt with the broad head of his cock. Pleasuring her with his body and all of his skill. Feeling the chill created by the Nightmares and his homesickness melt from the heat of her response.

She began to whimper and writhe, straining in his arms, voicing breathless pleas, ". . . yes . . . oh god . . . deeper . . ."

He caught her nipple in his fingers and pinched it, tugged it. Her inner muscles rippled along his length making him groan.

"That's it," he praised, completely infatuated by her response. She was totally focused on him, as he was on her, which was perfect. *She* was perfect.

Stacey fell apart in his embrace with a thready cry that almost set him off. He clenched his jaw and held back, gentling her with kisses and murmurs of appreciation.

"Jesus," she gasped, her head falling to the side to press her cheek to his. "Three orgasms in an hour. Are you trying to kill me?"

"Are you complaining? I can try harder."

She smacked his hand when he tweaked her nipple and he laughed.

"I like your laugh," she said shyly.

"I like you."

"You don't know me."

"Hmm . . . I know you love your son and you're a good friend to Lyssa. I know you're tough and you raised a child alone without any support, something you resent and rightfully so. You're uninhibited and comfortable in your skin. You've got a wicked sense of humor and you don't trust men to want you for more than sex."

"Sometimes that's convenient." She giggled, and the girlish sound combined with her lush woman's body made him even harder. "Jesus. You might want to get that thing checked."

"I've only had one orgasm to your three," he pointed out. "And I want you for more than sex."

She stiffened.

"I have no friends here, Stacey. Besides Aidan."

"Listen . . ." She struggled up to a seated position and lifted off of him.

Sighing inwardly with disappointment, Connor rose, too, and reached down to tug off the annoying condom. Such precautions weren't necessary in the Twilight where diseases did not exist and reproduction had to be planned, but he couldn't tell her that. She wouldn't believe him.

"Friends-with-benefits is a great arrangement for a lot of people. But not for me."

He took a moment to step into the nearby downstairs guest bathroom and disposed of the condom. "Okay . . ."

He lifted the toilet seat and began pissing with the door open, waiting for her to finish voicing her objection.

Stacey leaned against the jamb and watched him warily. Relieving himself in plain sight was base and a bit crude, but also undeniably intimate, which was what he wanted. Intimacy. Connection. He'd take it anyway he could get it. It also appeared to fascinate her enough to forget that she was naked from the waist down, a view he appreciated immensely.

"I can't decide if you're completely rude and arrogant," she murmured, almost to herself, "which I hate. Or if you're simply open and confident, which I like."

"You like me."

She snorted and crossed her arms over her chest. "I don't know you near as well as you think you know me. The only thing really working in your favor is that you're best friends with Aidan, who is overall a nice guy."

Connor stuck out his lower lip in a mock pout. "The three orgasms don't help?"

The corner of her mouth twitched and he was suddenly determined to make her laugh out loud. She was too serious, and he couldn't shake the feeling that the exterior shell protected a vulnerable middle. A middle that very few people were ever privileged enough to see.

"We shouldn't have done that," she said.

He flushed the toilet and then moved to the sink to wash up. He studied Stacey's reflection in the mirror. Their eyes met and held, "Why not?"

"Because our best friends are getting married. You and I are going to run into each other occasionally and this," she waved a hand between them, "is always going to be there.

That we know sexual things about each other. That I've seen you take a leak."

Pulling the towel off the rack, Connor dried his hands and then leaned back into the counter. "You don't remain friends with the people you sleep with?"

She bit her swollen lower lip. He wasn't a kissing man usually, but the desire to feel that mouth against his had been undeniable and he'd indulged. Stacey had full, plush lips. Connor wanted to feel them everywhere. All over his body.

At the thought, his cock, which was already at half-mast from the clenching of Stacey's recent orgasm, leaped to attention.

"Okay." She pointed an accusing finger at his waving erection. "That thing is a sexual lunatic."

Connor laughed and then fell silent when she joined him. The sound wasn't what he had expected. Instead of a girlish trill, it was low and throaty, almost rusty sounding, rarely used. Her green eyes sparkled and her cheeks flushed.

"Beautiful," he said.

She looked aside, then she turned away, moving back into the dining room to collect her discarded clothes. She held them to her torso in an obviously defensive posture and he took up her abandoned position of leaning against the jamb.

"You didn't answer my question," he murmured, watching her intently.

Shrugging, she said, "I have bad taste in men."

He didn't say anything to that, just considered her carefully.

"I'm going to take a shower." She moved to walk past him.

He reached out and caught her arm, stopping her. "Stacey."

Her gaze rested first on where his hand wrapped around her upper arm, then it lifted to meet his. Her brows rose.

"Do you like Chinese food?"

She blinked and then gifted him with a soft smile, recognizing the olive branch. "Moo shu pork. And cream cheese wontons."

"Got it."

There was a slight hesitation, then she nodded and moved to the stairs.

Connor knew what would happen next. She would come down washed and dressed, an outward show of her inward decision to wipe the slate clean. She would want to start over and pretend as if they'd just met and never fucked. He knew because it was how he handled similar situations in the Twilight. Early morning training had worked for centuries as an excuse not to spend the night. He wished Stacey had given them more time to be lovers, but he respected her decision and even thought she might be right. Better to end this as a quick, unplanned rut than to risk a messy situation.

By nature the Elite avoided emotional attachments. Very few of the Warriors partnered and those who did rarely stayed that way. Detachment was required to succeed and for those Guardians who were unfortunate enough to fall in love with an Elite, it was a lonely and unequal romance. The Elite were incapable of giving as much love as they received. In addition, for Connor it was simply bred into him to keep his focus on his mission.

"The Bruces live and die by the sword." He repeated the familiar refrain aloud. There was no other way.

That was why he was especially suited to protecting sensual Dreamers. It was a symbiotic relationship. He could don a fantasy and connect to another individual, fulfilling their dream while satisfying his own need for affection. A few hours of being the love of someone's life was enough to ease the chill of a house and bed he shared with no one else.

Blowing out his breath, Connor straightened and moved into the kitchen where he found the drawer that Lyssa and Aidan used to hold their take-out menus. They ate at Peony's Chinese Restaurant so often they had an account there, a bit of information Connor knew because he'd visited with Aidan in the dream state.

When a Guardian connected with a slipstream, all of the Dreamer's memories became an open book. Everything stored in Aidan's brain was now stored in Connor's. It had been a brutal acclimation at first, the rush of centuries of recollections—both Aidan's and the thousands of Dreamers Aidan had protected. Connor had learned to concentrate on the brightest moments in order to save his own sanity.

Of course, the brightest moments in Aidan's life were those he spent with Lyssa, which had forced Connor to experience what it felt like to be deeply in love with a woman. For centuries he had been the recipient of such overwhelming affection in fantasies. When he shared Aidan's dreams, he discovered what it was like to give that love back.

Connor pulled out the menu he wanted and closed the drawer. Something warm and soft rubbed against his ankles, and he glanced down to find JB circling his bare feet. It was then he realized that he was still naked. It was a state he was quite comfortable with when he was home alone. However, he was fairly certain it would make Stacey anxious, so he dropped the menu on the granite countertop and decided to borrow something of Aidan's to wear.

He reached the top of the stairs just as the upper floor guest bathroom door opened. Stacey emerged into the short hallway engulfed in a cloud of fragrant steam. Her hair was wrapped up in a white turban and her curvy body was hidden beneath a matching towel. She lifted her head and saw him—all of him. Her eyes dropped down to where the cat rolled shamelessly around his feet and then rose up to his eyes, stopping at all the places that heated and hardened under her perusal.

For his part, Connor enjoyed the view with equal pleasure. Her satiny skin was flushed pink from both the shower and the therapeutic effects of sexual release. Her thickly lashed green eyes were bright as jade, her full lips reddened, her breasts accentuated by the knotting of the towel between them.

Suddenly his decision to remain aloof and give her the space she wanted was trampled by the more pressing desire to feel her arching beneath him. He had no one in this plane he could talk to. No one with whom to share the details of his hellacious day, no Dreamer to lose himself in, no Elite to strategize with. He had no idea if he would ever go home again. But for a while, Stacey had enabled him to forget all of that. She had given him reason to smile and something else to focus on—her.

Just as he was focused on her now.

He gestured to the master bedroom across the hall. "I was going to find something to wear."

She nodded. "I'll be down in just a minute."

"Okay," he said lamely, arrested by the weird feelings he was experiencing.

Turning, Stacey walked to the door of the guestroom she was occupying. Connor didn't move, riveting by the gentle, unaffected sway of her perfect ass. Stacey turned the knob and stepped a short way into the room.

"You're staring," she tossed over her shoulder before disappearing from view behind the closing door.

"I know," he muttered. He continued staring long after he heard the click of the latch.

Chapter 6

The coast on a balmy night was always beautiful. This evening was no exception, but Aidan was too focused on his mission to enjoy the soft silver lighting of the full moon or the music of the ocean tide. With silent steps, he rounded the corner of the motel, heading toward Room 108. There were people everywhere—groups of twenty-somethings who were dressed for the clubs and carrying booze in their hands, and older couples strolling toward the beach.

He wasn't worried about the number of possible witnesses. Pretty much "anything goes" seemed to be the rule around here. Shit, he was fairly certain he could ask someone to help him break into the room. A simple story about losing his key while in a compromising situation would work. But the ruse wasn't necessary. Aidan had simply jimmied the lock to the housekeeping office door, which was conveniently hidden from guest view, and snagged the master key.

Armed with the required accessory, he simply walked casually, whistling, his hands in his pockets and his thoughts with Lyssa, who waited in the car with a fully loaded Glock in her lap. In his mind's eye, he could see her—her lush mouth set in grim lines, her dark eyes hard and wary. He loved that she was compassionate and gentle by nature, but tough, smart, and willing to do whatever was necessary to keep them both alive.

He'd shared enough romance novel-based fantasies with Dreamers to know that not all women would manage their situation with as much practicality. Some would wail and cry and wait to be rescued.

Aidan paused before the correct door, noting the lack of light emanating from behind the curtains covering the large window. No one home. He was both pleased and not. At least if the Guardian had been inside, he would know her location. As it was, she could be anywhere. Or she could be somewhere—such as near Lyssa.

Withdrawing the key from his pocket, Aidan slipped it into the lock and turned. The mechanism tumbled open. He thrust the door wide and flicked the switch on the wall. The light on the table between the two beds came on, revealing one mattress covered in the spilled contents of a duffle bag and another pristinely made up. A little further past the sleeping area was a sink, mirror, and door to the bathroom.

The room was empty.

Stepping inside, Aidan shut the door behind him and kicked his foot at the bed skirt. The toe of his boot connected with hollow-sounding plywood, a cheaper alternative to traditional metal bed frames. No one could hide under the beds. He then moved toward the bathroom, checking there for possible ambush, before finally moving to the items of interest on the mattress—a comm unit, an assortment of maps and knives, and a data chip, which unfortunately lacked a reader. Aidan took it all anyway, tossing everything back into the duffle. As he thrust his hand into the bag, he touched something hard and cold. His pulse rate leaped. He wrapped his fingers around the stem and withdrew it.

The *taza*. And inside that, something wrapped carefully in thick cloth. He pulled out the small bundle and opened it, finding a metallic object encrusted with dried dirt. Rubbing with his fingertips, Aidan revealed delicate filigree scrollwork. He had no idea what it was and wouldn't know until it was thoroughly cleaned, but its importance was obvious to his trained eye. He rewrapped it and slipped it into his pocket, then returned his attention to the *taza*.

It looked just as it did in the renderings in the Elders' journal. A silver-like metal scarred by centuries, dented and bearing empty settings where jewels once decorated the lip. What purpose it served, he hadn't yet figured out, but it was his. In his possession. His mouth curved in a genuine smile that reflected the tiny sense of accomplishment he felt. He was another step closer to the truth. A truth that would hopefully set Lyssa free.

A quick search of the drawers and closet came up with little else. Some clothes and more spiked jewelry, like he'd seen the Guardian wearing earlier. Still no reader for the data chip. Sorry-assed luck, but something was better than nothing.

He looped the long handle of the bag over his shoulder and turned toward the door just as a key was heard pushing into the lock. Aidan froze for a heartbeat, his mind swiftly noting that the lights were on and clearly visible from the outside. Dropping the bag, he crouched, preparing.

The door flew open in an explosion of movement and sound. His adversary lunged straight for him, her movements visible only as a blur of red hair and flowing black skirts. A scream of frightening volume and pitch rent the air, startling him and galvanizing him into action. Aidan sprung upward just as her body would have hit his. The opposing velocity of his attack jarred them both, the brutal impact forcing a grunt from him and a cry of something akin to rage from her.

They hit the floor in a tangle of limbs. She was swinging punches and he was right there with her, fighting back, refusing to allow his brain to acknowledge her gender. It was her or him. He couldn't look at the altercation any other way.

She rolled him to his back, levering her torso up with one hand so that she could free her other for a downward punch. It was then that Aidan caught a quick glimpse of her face. A brief flash, but that was enough to shock him into stillness. Stunned, he didn't deflect her swing, taking the full force of her fist in his jaw.

The bite of pain snapped him out of his horror. Feet flat to the floor, he bucked his hips upward, tossing her over his head. He rolled to his stomach and crawled atop her kicking feet, absorbing her barrage of blows with gritted teeth. His arm drew back and punched hard to her temple. It was an assault that would have knocked a large man out cold. The redhead only bared her fangs and hissed like a wild animal.

"What the hell?" Aidan growled, struggling to restrain the feral Guardian.

Together, they crashed into the nearby dresser hard enough to bang the furniture into the wall. Her nails tore at the exposed flesh of his forearms and snared his shirt. The barrage was unlike anything Aidan had ever experienced in centuries of living. The woman was possessed, unrelenting, and somehow tapping into some power that allowed her to continue when anyone else would be unconscious.

In the end, he had only one choice.

Grimly determined, Aidan fought to maneuver into position and encircled her head with his arms. Then, twisting like he would a twist-top beer, he attempted to snap her neck. A task that should have taken less than a minute, except she was unbelievably strong and snarling like a mad beast. White hot pain seared deep into his leg, giving him the final adrenaline surge he needed to wrench her neck far enough. The splintering of her spinal cord reverberated through the room. The resulting dearth of noise—broken only by his gasping, labored breathing—was chilling.

Aidan stared down at the lifeless body in his arms, still mentally grappling with her eyes, which were solid black with no pupils or irises for relief, and her teeth, which were jagged and wickedly sharp within the gaping hole of her mouth.

Whatever the hell she was, she wasn't a Guardian. That was for damn sure.

Aidan pushed to his feet and then stumbled back down onto one knee with a curse. Looking at his leg, he saw the dagger embedded there, explaining the vicious spear of pain he'd felt earlier.

"Damn it!"

Yanking the blade free of his thigh, Aidan ripped off a strip of the redhead's flowing black cotton skirt and tied it around as a makeshift bandage. He would be fully healed by morning, but he had the interim to get through.

"Shit." He glared at the dead *thing* on the floor. "How the fuck am I going to carry you out of here with my leg like this?"

But he couldn't leave her behind. She wasn't human, and he couldn't be indicted for murder.

Aidan pushed to standing again, leaning heavily against the television while the room spun. He was heaving in oxygen as if he'd run a damn marathon and now that the adrenal rush was abating slightly, he was becoming aware of the multitude of scratches and minor scrapes that wounded him. His leg hurt like hell, too.

Reaching down, he grabbed the duffle again. Then he slung the dead weight of his unwanted burden over his shoulder and exited the room.

He was several doors down when a group of dressed-to-impress young men rounded the corner in front of him and asked, "What's going on, man?"

"I told her to quit after the fifth shot," he explained, slowing his pace. "She wouldn't listen. It all went to shit after that. I'm just hoping I make it to our room before she pukes down my back."

"Sucks to be you," commiserated one of the guys. "The clubs are just starting to rock and your night is done. No pussy for you either, unless you ditch her."

"I wish I could," he said, meaning every word.

The rest of the group laughed and suggested he "leave the bitch at home next time."

"Good idea," he muttered, continuing on.

It was a long hike from the room back to the rented dark green Honda Civic, a damn sight longer than the trip from the car to the room.

Lyssa hopped out upon seeing his approach, engaging the safety on the Glock before quickly tucking it into the waistband at the back of her jean shorts. Her shoulder-blade-length blonde hair was restrained in a ponytail and her taut abdomen was displayed by the cropped white T-shirt she wore. Her face was scrubbed clean and free of cosmetics, and Aidan was positive he'd never seen anything or anyone as beautiful in his life. He didn't regret anything he had to do to keep her safe.

"Oh my god." She blinked rapidly. "You're *kidnapping* her?"

"Something like that." He grunted as he stumbled over the uneven dirt road.

"What's wrong? Oh shit! Your leg's bleeding."

"Open the back door, Hot Stuff."

"Don't 'hot stuff' me," she muttered, even as she hurried to obey him. "You're not supposed to get hurt!"

"Yeah, well, it's better than being dead like our friend here."

He could feel the wave of horror and confusion that moved through Lyssa.

"Jesus . . . she's *dead?* And you're putting her in the car?" She stood frozen, watching him arrange their passenger lengthwise across the seat. "What the hell am I saying?"

she said finally, the high pitch of her voice the only sign of how deeply disturbed she was. "We have to take her with us. We can't leave her here, can we?"

"No, we can't." Aidan backed out of the cramped backseat and straightened to face her. She was pale, her eyes too big, her lips colorless. For the first time, she was confronted with irrefutable proof of what he was—a warrior who killed as necessary. "Are you okay?"

Lyssa inhaled sharply, her gaze darting to the body in the car. Then she nodded. "Yeah."

"Are *we* okay?" he asked grimly.

She frowned, staring at him. Then her face cleared. "Yes. We're okay. I know you did this for me. For us. It was either you or her, right?"

"Right." He wanted to touch her, to stroke her cheek, and to pull her close enough to breathe in the scent of her skin. But he felt dirty, and he didn't want to put his hands on her until he was clean.

"Well, she's not the one I'm in love with, so you made the right choice."

He heaved out a relieved little laugh, the tension draining from his body. "She had the *taza*, too, which is really fucking convenient since we're not going to make it down to Ensenada."

As she regained her composure, her chin lifted and her shoulders went back. "Should I get out the supplies?"

They'd been cautious and brought along a medical bag of emergency items. Their life together was a dangerous one and neither of them ever forgot that.

"Not here," he said. His injury recovery time was rapid compared to humans, but he'd discovered that a stitch here and there could cut several hours of healing down to one or two. "Let's head back toward the border. We'll stop somewhere private."

There was an Army-issue shovel in the trunk, part of a kit he'd picked up at the local military surplus store. He knew Lyssa was thinking of it, too.

"What about the statue for McDougal?"

"I'll tell him I was mugged and got injured, which cut our trip short."

Lyssa raised a brow. "You, big guy?"

Aidan shrugged. "He can't prove me wrong."

"Alright." She stepped back and opened the front passenger door for him. "Let's hurry."

Losing the battle to keep his distance, he pressed a kiss to her cheek before he gingerly attempted to get in the car.

"I love you," she said.

"Thank you." His gaze met hers. "I needed to hear that."

She blew him a kiss. "I know."

Within minutes, they were on the road heading north.

Stacey watched Connor spoon more Kung Pao chicken onto his plate. There were several mostly empty boxes of Chinese food scattered all across the coffee table. She set her chopsticks down and picked up a cream cheese wonton. "I have never seen anyone eat so much food in one sitting in my life," she said wryly.

He grinned that broad boyish smile that made her stomach flutter. "You're a pretty good eater, too," he said. "I dig it."

"My hips don't."

"Your hips don't know what's good for them."

"Ha."

Connor sent her a mock glare and expertly wielded chopsticks to convey a piece of chicken to his mouth. Her gaze dropped to his bared stomach and she admired the sheer masculine beauty of his six-pack abdomen. Even after eating enough food to feed her and Justin for a week, he still looked taut, lean, and hard.

Gorgeous.

She was still having trouble processing the fact that they'd had sex, although her body still tingled from the aftereffects. They were sitting cross-legged on the living room floor watching *The Mummy,* one of her favorite movies. She was a sucker for a blow 'em up action flick with a hot hero and a touch of romance. Connor said he liked it, too, but he spent more time watching her than he did the television. She'd have thought his interest would wane after the sex, at least a little. Instead he seemed more interested than before. She had to admit, she was intrigued by him, too.

"So why are you here?" she asked, setting her elbow on the table and her chin in her palm.

"I have some information for Aidan."

"You couldn't call?"

He shook his head with a smile. "I tried that. He doesn't remember a damn thing I tell him."

"How like a man," she teased.

"Watch it, sweetheart."

Stacey liked it when he called her that. There was something in the rich brogue that lent sincerity to the common endearment. "Are you ex-Special Forces like Aidan?"

"Yeah." There was a melancholy tinge to his response.

"You sound as if you miss it."

"I do." He reached over and snatched the half-eaten wonton from her plate and popped it into his mouth.

"Hey!" she protested, frowning. "There are fresh ones in the box."

"They don't taste as good."

Her eyes narrowed and he stuck a playful tongue out at her. On the screen, Rick O'Connell was battling against a mob of people with the plague. She watched the scene for a moment, then asked Connor, "So what do you do now that you're out of the army or wherever?"

"Same thing as Cross."

She'd tried to get Aidan to name an actual branch of the military and country affiliation, but he was tight-lipped. Lyssa said it was super-secret covert stuff.

So, what? Stacey had said. *If he tells me, he'll have to kill me?*

Lyssa laughed. *Of course not.*

'Cuz seriously, Stacey muttered, *the curiosity is killing me, Doc. He might as well tell me. That would be a kinder way to go.*

Of course, Aidan elected not to put her out of her misery. She knew Connor would be the same. He had a similar air of wariness about him, as if he was dreading the questions he knew were coming.

"You know," she said, "in romance novels the Special Forces heroes usually become high-tech security experts when they retire. Not . . . researchers . . . or personal shoppers."

Connor wiped his hands on a napkin and leaned back, supporting his weight on his arms behind him. He wore only loose-fitting striped pajama bottoms, leaving his torso bared to her perusal. His body was a finely honed machine, able to hold up her weight as if it were nothing. The impressive breadth of his shoulders rippled with muscle and his biceps. . .

Her mouth watered. Dear god, he was savagely beautiful. There was nothing tempered about him. Nothing refined. Even at rest, as he was now, she sensed an alertness to him, an inner coiling of power that left him always ready to pounce.

"You're staring," he purred, his blue eyes watching her with predatory intensity. She knew if she gave him even the tiniest bit of encouragement, he would have her on her back in a minute or less.

The image made her shiver.

"I know," she said, mimicking his earlier statement.

The corner of his shamelessly luscious mouth lifted in a half smile. "So . . . are you telling me that I'm not romance hero material because I don't install security systems?"

He was romance hero material, all right. At least on the outside. And in bed.

"I didn't say that." Stacey shrugged lamely and dragged her gaze back to the television. It was torture to look away from all that golden skin, but it was self-preservation, too. "I'm just saying that I wouldn't expect guys such as you and Aidan to be interested in hunting down old stuff for old guys with too much money. I'd think you would be bored after all the . . . excitement of what you used to do."

"The Black Market isn't without danger," he said softly.

"Anytime different people want the same thing, it can get ugly. If they want it bad enough, it can get deadly."

She glanced at him. "Doesn't sound like a dream job."

Connor's lips pursed a moment, then he said, "In my family, we all join the military. It's a given."

"Really?"

His shoulders lifted in a small shrug, which did wonderful things to his pectorals. "Really."

"So you never had something else you wanted to do?"

"I never considered anything else."

"That's sad, Connor."

The sound of his name spoken in her voice shocked them both. Stacey could tell it affected him, because he blinked rapidly and looked a little confused. For her part, she knew that the way she was thinking about him was far from friendly. It was obscene. She wanted to lick and nibble on all his yummy looking skin. His dark honey-hued hair was a little too long, curling over his nape and around the tops of his ears. She wanted to touch it. Run her fingers through it.

"What's your dream?" he asked, his intimate tone drawing her deeper under his spell. He gestured with his chin toward the dining table where her ridiculously expensive textbooks sat ignored. "Are you working toward it now?"

She almost said "yes" as part of her positive thinking overhaul she was working on. Instead, she revealed something she'd never even told Lyssa. "I wanted to be a writer," she confessed.

Twin brows raised in visible surprise. "A writer? What kind of writer?"

Stacey felt her face heat. "A romance writer."

"Really?" Now it was his turn to sound shocked. He did it really well, too.

"Yep."

"What happened?"

"Life happened."

"Huh . . ." He straightened, then startled her by stilling her fingers, which were restlessly spinning a fortune cookie around. The feel of his touch was warm and comforting. His hand was so large; it dwarfed hers. The man was at least twice her size, and yet he could be so gentle. "That's the last thing I would have guessed you would say."

"I know."

"You're so practical."

"I wish."

"Did you give up your dream?"

She stared at their physical connection, his skin so much darker than hers, the knuckles dusted with barely discernable golden strands of hair. "Sure. It was silly anyway."

Connor couldn't think of what to say to Stacey's dismissal of something that was obviously important to her. He wasn't a Nurturer or a Healer, and he wasn't a man who spent time talking to women. At least not words that weren't for the purposes of seduction. When women came to him, it wasn't conversation they wanted. The best he could manage in the way of comfort was to stroke the center of Stacey's soft palm with his callused thumb.

The chaste contact aroused him. When he brushed lower, across the pulse point in her wrist, the rapid beat of her heart betrayed how it aroused her, too. Neither of them acted upon the attraction, despite their quickening breaths. He was content to simply enjoy the soft thrumming of desire in his blood.

Then the phone rang and broke the moment.

She blinked, as if waking, then pushed to her feet. "Aidan called earlier when you were sleeping. It's probably him again."

Connor rose as well and followed her into the kitchen. Stacey picked up the handset, revealing the caller ID. *Best Western Big Bear.* The tension that gripped Stacey's small frame was palpable.

She hit the "talk" button and lifted the receiver to her ear. "Hi, baby."

He placed his hands on her slight shoulders and began to knead gently, fighting the tightening that threatened to knot the muscles.

"But you have school," she began, which resulted in a long barrage of argument from the other end of the line. "Yes, I know it's been a long time . . ." Her chest expanded and collapsed on a silent sigh. "Fine. You can come home Monday night."

The excitement elicited by Stacey's capitulation was audible through the receiver.

"Okay." She tried valiantly to sound cheerful. "I'm glad you're having a great time . . . I love you, too. Keep warm. Wear that scarf Lyssa bought you for Christmas." She managed a weak laugh. "Yeah, who knew you'd actually use the damn thing? Of course . . . Don't worry about me; I'm watching *The Mummy* . . . At least a hundred times, yes. So what? It's a good flick! Okay . . . Goodnight . . . Love you."

She hung up and the arm holding the handset fell to her side in a defeatist gesture.

"Hey," Connor murmured, caressing the length of her arm until he reached the phone. He tugged it from nerveless fingers and set it on the breakfast bar. "It's okay. He'll be back soon."

"That's just it," she said, turning to face him only because he caught her shoulders and forced her to. "I don't know if he will come back, or if he'll stay with me when he does."

He stared down at her unhappy face with its pink-tipped nose and turned down mouth. Cupping her cheek, he brushed his thumb across her cheekbone.

"He's fourteen years old," she said mournfully. "He wants a dad, a man he can emulate and learn from. Tommy lives in Hollywood, where it's glamorous and there's something going on every minute. Justin hates it here in the Valley. He says it's boring, and for kids his age, I know it is. I moved to Murrieta because it was cheap at the time—I could buy a house and save on my taxes—and because it's quiet. There isn't much around here that can lure a teen-age boy into trouble."

"See?" he said. "A practical woman, just as I said."

A brave woman. A strong woman. A woman he admired.

She faked a smile and it hit him like a punch to the gut. He hated the façade for his benefit. He wanted her all, the real deal. Connor Bruce, best known as "the guy with whom you don't get emotional," wanted Stacey's emotions.

"If Tommy decides he wants to try being a father full-time," she continued tearfully, "Justin will go. Tommy is as much a kid as Justin; they'd have a blast together."

Her head fell forward, hiding her features in a mass of dark curls. "Tommy would probably sue me for child support, too, which would make his life easier. And even if he didn't, I would still send them money. God only knows how they would eat otherwise. One meal a day on the set? *If* Tommy's lucky enough to be working for once!"

A soft sob rent the air and Connor did the only thing he could do; he caught her chin in his fingers and lifted her mouth to fit his kiss. It was a gentle offer of comfort, just lips, no tongue. He took nothing from her and offered consolation the only way he knew how. "You're getting ahead of yourself, sweetheart," he murmured, nuzzling her nose with his.

"I'm sorry." Stacey kissed him back, tiny kisses. Sweet kisses. "I'm a basket case today. Hormones or something. I swear I am not normally like this."

"It's okay."

Surprisingly, it was.

Stepping back slightly, Connor bent and caught her up behind the knees and lifted her into his arms. He carried her out of the dining room and back into the living room, where he sank into the down-filled couch with her in his lap. She fit perfectly there, her lush body settling warmly against his bare skin. He tucked her head under his chin and rocked her.

Taking and giving. The connection he'd sought and needed so desperately earlier, reestablished without sex and yet strengthened by their earlier frantic mating. Having gotten the animal lust out of the way, they'd exposed the other feelings, laying them out in the open between them. Understood and shared.

"Thank you," she whispered wearily, curling tighter against him.

Soon, her shallow, rhythmic breathing told him she was connected to the Twilight. She was at his home, where he longed to be. Dreaming.

He hoped it was of him.

Chapter 7

Connor traversed the length of the rock-lined hallway to the main cavern with an impatient stride. As he drew closer to the grotto, the air grew more humid due to the large body of water that waited just beyond the craggy edge. There was a mildewy, mossy smell that permeated the air and made him long for his life of just weeks ago. A life above ground with women, beer, and a damn good fight when he needed one.

And a door for an entrance and exit. That would be nice.

He wasn't looking forward to the necessary dip in the icy water of the lake. It was near torture to make the ascent to the surface when one's lungs were seized by the frigid temperature. Unlike everything else in the Twilight, the water in the lake could not be altered by mere thought. No amount of wishing, ordering, or hoping made the liquid any more bearable.

So he simply saluted his men, checked to make certain that his glaive was secured in the scabbard crossing his back, and dove in.

Long moments later, Connor emerged freezing and gasping, crawling up the sandy bank while wracked by violent shivers. He

*was struck by a feeling of déjà vu so disconcerting that he didn't re-
alize he wasn't alone until he was tackled and knocked backward.*

*As a smaller, wirier body wrapped around his, his roar of out-
rage reflected off the surface of the water and released his mounting
tension. Connor twisted and grappled with his assailant until the
moment they both fell back into the lake in an explosion of water
and slapping skin. He grabbed his assailant by the scruff of his
robes and dragged him onto the shore.*

"Wait!" *Sheron cried.*

*Connor reached over his shoulder and pulled his glaive free of its
scabbard.* "We've been through this before, old man," *he growled.*

"We did not conclude our discussion."

"So start talking before I lose what's left of my patience."

The Elder pushed back his soaked cowl. "Remember what I told
you about the slipstreams we established in the Temple?"

"Yeah."

"And how the only location in the Twilight that is secure from
Nightmares is the cavern you have commandeered?"

"Yes."

"Nightmares infiltrated the Temple streams, Bruce, melding
with the Guardian in transit to form one being."

"Fuck me." *Connor's grip on his glaive tightened and sweat
dotted his brow.* "Can they travel by themselves? Are the humans
in trouble now? Have we finally screwed them all the way by in-
fecting their world as well as their dreams?"

"Not so far as we know. Unlike the slipstreams in the cavern,
these are opened only briefly, just long enough to make the jump.
Then they are closed again."

"How did you figure out what was happening?"

"We began by sending a guard through in a rapid cycle—in
and out."

Connor began to pace.

"It became apparent over time that some of the guards were not well," Sheron continued. "At first we assumed it was due to the location."

"Being outside the cavern."

"Yes. Then they began to change. Physically. Emotionally. Mentally. Eliciting fear and sadness in those around them seemed to be very important to them. They grew more violent and cruel. Their eyes began to change color. They stopped eating."

"Oh man . . ."

"We realized then what had happened. The Nightmares inside them were taking over, urging the Guardian into acts of terror so they could feed off those negative emotions."

Since the Nightmares had discovered the human subconscious through the fissure created by the Elders, they'd been using the power of the human mind as sustenance. Fear, fury, misery—these were easily aroused through dreams and fed Nightmares so well.

Lowering his sword, Connor freed one hand to scrub at his jaw. "How many of those things are there?"

"There were a dozen in the original trial, but only one affected Guardian remained alive and you killed him today."

"Be thankful for small favors, eh?" Connor snorted.

Sheron removed the scabbard belt from his too-lean waist and emptied the water that had collected inside it. Then he sheathed his glaive and moved to a nearby rock, leaving a trail of droplets in his wake.

"What aren't you telling me?" Connor followed with glaive in hand. He didn't trust Sheron as far as he could throw him. Not any more. Sad, considering he had once trusted the man with his life.

"What I came here to tell you." The Elder settled onto a large rock and spread out his sodden robes as much as possible. "The trial was deemed a success before the symptoms of Nightmare possession began to present themselves. We were testing for successful round-trips, not side-effects. An additional contingent of guards and Elders were sent through before we understood the extent of the problem."

Connor's gut tightened into a hard knot. "Well, yank them all back, damn it!"

"We cannot. By the time we comprehended the error, the Guardians had altered so much they were incapable of returning upon their threads. They were no longer the same individuals who departed. We were able to retrieve only the unaffected ones."

"What the hell have you done? How many of those things are out there?"

"Ten of the lot were unable to return. We have sent twenty more through since then. A gamble. Those who are unaffected will hunt those who are and put them down. Cross will expect the Guardians to search for him, but there is no way for him to know about the hybrids."

Before the rebellion, Aidan had been Captain and Connor had been his lieutenant. Together, they had run the Elite with faultless precision. Life had seemed so simple then. Now, everything was complicated.

"Why are you telling me this?" Connor asked suspiciously.

"Cross's death is not something I want."

"But you want the Key dead," Connor argued. "And you'll have to kill Cross to get to the Key, I promise you that."

"We will manage that when the time comes."

"Like hell you will!" Connor launched himself like a missile, flying through the air and slamming into the Elder's chest with his shoulder.

The Elder would make a great hostage.
They tumbled, rolling across the sand—

Gasping, Connor jolted awake, which also woke the warm curvy woman lying in his arms.

"Hey." Stacey's voice was husky from sleep. In the faint glow from the muted television, he saw her head turn toward him. They lay on the sofa; him against the back, her against him. "Are you alright? Did you have a nightmare?"

He pushed up and climbed over her carefully. "Yeah."

"Want me to make you some hot tea or something?"

"No." Bending, he kissed her forehead. "Go back to sleep. I just remembered something important and I better write it down before I forget it again."

Connor moved over to the breakfast bar, turned on the recessed spotlights above it, and grabbed the notepad he'd seen there earlier. Then he pulled a chair back from the dining table, borrowed the mechanical pencil lying atop Stacey's textbooks, and turned his attention to finding a clean sheet of paper.

As he flipped through pages of lovingly drawn renderings of Aidan, Connor's heartbeat slowed. His breathing deepened and became more regular. The pictures of Aidan before him were not of the same Aidan he'd been fighting alongside for centuries. The Aidan captured by Lyssa in detailed pencil lines appeared younger and happier. His eyes were bright and the lines of strain less apparent.

Connor studied the images for long moments, then he heard movement on the couch. He pivoted to find Stacey curled on her side, her eyelids fluttering as she drifted back to sleep.

He smiled, once again noting how the chill created by his dreams faded just because she was near. It was amazing what the feeling of female comfort could do for a man. He could see how Aidan's relationship with Lyssa had changed his friend in wondrous ways.

Which only made Connor more determined to succeed in his mission.

He was here for a reason. His actions in this plane of existence would keep the people he cared about safe. It also kept the promise he'd made long ago—to protect the Dreamers from the mistakes of the Elders.

Refocused on his task, Connor returned his attention to the blank paper before him and tried to collect his thoughts.

Aidan didn't remember the conversations they'd had in his dreams. There was no reason for Connor to think that his own brain was any different, which meant the two "meetings" with Sheron were products of his imagination.

Still, despite knowing how dreams worked, he had a very hard time believing that the fantastical story Sheron had told him was a product of his mind. He didn't think up shit like that. He considered himself more brawn than brain.

Unless the Elders had a way the Guardians didn't know about. . . .Or perhaps Wager had gleaned more information from the data chip?

Confused and a bit horrified by the many possibilities— not the least of which was the idea that what he'd dreamed might be the truth—Connor began to write.

*   *   *

It was the sound of a door opening and the distant rumbling of a garage opener motor that woke Stacey. Groggy and too comfortable for words, it took her a minute to comprehend where she was. Scrubbing at heavy-lidded eyes with her fists, she shifted a little and found herself wrapped in a heavy cocoon of large, sleepy male.

Her brain geared up slowly, piece-by-piece registering the heavy arm and leg that were slung across her, the soft lips and warm breath that caressed her shoulder, the morning hard-on that poked insistently into her buttocks. They were on the couch in the living room, spooned on their sides, Connor's chin above the top of her head, his big body half draped over hers. She normally needed a thick blanket to stay warm, but his body heat resembled a blast furnace at her back. Despite her silky spaghetti-strap pajama top and matching pants bottoms, she wasn't cold at all.

Blinking, Stacey looked through the dining room into the kitchen and discovered two faces bearing equally shocked expressions staring back at her. "Uh . . ."

Horrified at the thought of Connor smelling her morning breath, Stacey snapped her mouth shut and attempted to extricate herself from his embrace. He was dressed, too, of course, but that didn't make the situation any less embarrassing. There was no way they'd ever be able to pretend that nothing had happened between them.

Connor's response to her wiggling was a grumbled protest and a large hand cupping her breast. Her nipple, shamelessly happy with the attention, puckered wantonly into his palm, which set off a now predictable reaction in his cock.

"Umm . . ." he purred, snuggling closer and rocking his hips against hers suggestively.

Aidan and Lyssa's mouths fell open.

Stacey winced and smacked at Connor's hand. "Stop that!" she hissed. "They're home."

She could tell the moment the information sunk in. He stiffened against her, then muttered a barely audible curse. Lifting his head, he looked over her shoulder and said, "Cross."

"Bruce," Aidan returned tightly.

Wincing, Stacey rolled out of Connor's now lax embrace and landed unceremoniously on her hands and knees on the floor between the coffee table and the couch. Connor straightened into a seated position.

"You guys are back early," she said with mock cheerfulness as Connor rose and pulled her up with him. "How was your trip?" Breeze on through the storm, she thought. It usually worked, at least temporarily.

"I was stabbed in the leg," Aidan muttered.

"I helped bury some freak of nature." Lyssa shuddered.

It was Stacey's turn to gape. Her eyes dropped to the thick white bandage that peeked out from the bottom of Aidan's nearly knee-length shorts.

"Oh my god," she said, rushing around the coffee table before her lack of a bra penetrated her consciousness. Her face heated, and she wrapped her arms across her chest. A heartbeat later the chenille throw that decorated Lyssa's couch was being draped around her shoulders. She glanced up at Connor gratefully.

He offered her a grim smile. "Go upstairs and change," he said, looking over her head at Aidan.

"I'll go with you," Lyssa said quickly. "I need a shower something fierce."

Stacey looked at her boss and frowned, noting the pale skin and the dark circles under brown eyes. Lyssa hadn't looked so tired since before Aidan came into her life.

"Sure thing, Doc." Stacey waited for her friend to join her before heading toward the staircase. Connor remained where he was, standing tall and proud despite his own state of undress. His gaze never left Aidan's.

Lyssa barely made it to the upstairs landing before whispering, "You *slept* with him? *Already?*"

Wincing, Stacey said, "What makes you think that?"

An arched brow was Lyssa's reply.

"Okay, okay." Stacey pulled Lyssa into the master bedroom and shut the door.

"That's so not like you, Stace!"

"I know. It just . . . happened."

Lyssa plopped down on the edge of the mattress and glanced around the room. "Where's Justin?"

"Not in here," Stacey muttered, running a hand through her rat's nest hairdo. She always looked like crap in the morning. Just how she'd want the hottest guy she had ever seen to see her.

"Obviously," Lyssa said dryly.

Once, the room had been decorated in varying shades of blue in an effort to help Lyssa sleep. Now it was decorated Oriental-style, with a massive standing shoji screen placed before the sliding glass door to the left of the bed and black towels with gold embroidered kanji characters on them in the open bathroom on the right. A bright red satin dragon comforter covered the bed, and the mattress was framed in intricately carved wood and topped with a lacquered multi-paneled painting on the wall.

It was an exotic and unique bedroom, sensual and seductive. Very different from the soft taupe that decorated the rest of the condo, or the Victorian-era theme of the veterinary clinic. Prior to meeting Aidan, Stacey would never have imagined her friend in such surroundings, but it suited the woman Lyssa had become. As Caucasian as she was—and Lyssa was about as Barbie perfect as a girl could get with dark, almond-shaped eyes—the international flavor of the room spoke to an adventurous side Stacey hadn't known about.

"Tommy came into some money," Stacey said. "He picked up Justin and took him to Big Bear for the week-end."

Lyssa blinked. "Oh, wow!"

"Yeah, that was my reaction, too."

"When was the last time they saw each other?"

"Five years ago." Stacey dropped into the wooden-backed chair by the door. "So how was your mini-vacation?"

Shaking her head, Lyssa said, "Oh no, you're not chang-ing the subject that easily."

"Hey, you had a funeral for a freak of nature!" Stacey protested. "That's way more interesting than my sex life."

"It wasn't a funeral; it was roadkill," Lyssa muttered, toeing off her mud stained white Vans and stretching lengthwise across the end of the bed with her head propped on her hand. "We couldn't leave it there. It was . . . *gross*."

The horror in Lyssa's voice roused exasperation in Stacey. Too much was too much.

"I know you love animals and all, Doc, but pulling over to bury roadkill is just nasty."

"Let's get back to the topic of you *doing* the nasty," Lyssa said with undisguised eagerness.

Stacey laughed. "This is so high school."

"Isn't it? So what happened?"

Blowing out an exasperated breath, Stacey gave up trying to be evasive and began to explain what she didn't quite understand.

"Man," Aidan muttered, scowling. "Your night with Stacey is going to come back and bite me in the ass."

Connor's jaw tightened and his arms crossed his chest. No way in hell was he getting chastised for his private business. "I hate to tell you this, Cross, but my sex life has nothing to do with you."

Cursing under his breath, Aidan cleared a spot amid Stacey's textbooks on the dining table and set a black duffle bag down. "When your sex life includes Lyssa's best friend, it does."

"Oh? How so?"

Aidan shot him an arch glance over his shoulder. "Here's how it will go: You're going to piss Stacey off for one reason or another. She's going to complain to Lyssa. Lyssa will complain to me. I'll say, 'Leave me out of it.' And she's going to say, 'You're sleeping on the couch.'"

"You're leaping to conclusions."

"Conclusions based on historical knowledge," Aidan said, unzipping the bag and withdrawing the contents one by one. "That's why I stopped double-dating with you, remember? One of us would fuck up and we'd both end up paying."

"This is different."

"Yeah, it's worse. I've got Lyssa for the long haul, Lyssa's got Stacey for the long haul, and Stacey has good reason not to trust men. She's got a taste for guys like you."

"What is that supposed to mean, dickhead?" Connor growled.

"Lyssa told me Stacey has a history of hooking up with men who don't stick around." Aidan pulled a metal cup out of the duffle and set it gingerly on the table. Considering the thing looked the worse for wear, Connor understood it was important.

He stepped closer to check it out.

"When I first got here," Aidan continued, still emptying the bag, "Stacey was so wary of Lyssa getting hurt, she lent her a pepper spray pen. Told her to shoot me with it if I turned out to be an alien or something weird."

"Huh?" Connor picked up the cup and examined it. "She knew you were an alien?"

"No." Holding up a data chip, Aidan asked, "Did you bring a reader with you?" At Connor's negative head shake, he cursed and dropped it on the polished wood surface.

"What's up with the alien reference then?" Connor was confused.

"It was a joke. Stacey's got a twisted sense of humor."

"Oh." Connor grinned and put the cup back.

"The point is, she *armed* Lyssa against me, because she was worried I'd hurt her somehow. She's tough."

"Yeah." She was. Connor knew that. He also knew she was tender and vulnerable. He'd seen a glimpse beneath the shell. "I like that about her."

Aidan tossed the now empty duffel onto one of the

dining chairs. "You won't like it so much when she sprays you in the eyeballs with that shit."

Resting one palm flat on the tabletop, Connor leaned over and said, "You're pissing me off, Cross. Why are you so damn sure I'm going to fuck her over?"

"When have you ever been interested in settling down with one woman?" Aidan shot back. "I've known you for centuries. You've never wanted anything more involved than getting laid."

"Neither did you," Connor retorted.

"Obviously, I've changed."

"And I suppose—according to you—I never will?"

"What are you talking about?" Aidan snapped. "Why are we arguing about this? Just leave her alone. That shouldn't be difficult for you. It's not as if you're hard up."

"Thanks for the glowing endorsement." Snorting, Connor reached for the cloth bundle. "Not that it's any of your damn business, but I wanted to spend more time getting to know Stacey. *She* blew *me* off. Don't worry about my feelings, though. I don't have any."

If he hadn't been in a bad mood, Connor might have found amusement in Aidan's disbelieving glance. But he felt shitty and so it wasn't funny. It sucked. The whole thing sucked. "Forget it, Cross," he grumbled. "I can't change what's already been done and it was over before it started."

"Good." Aidan watched him unwrap the linen and reveal a grimy, dirt-covered blob.

"What is this?"

"Hell if I know. We'll clean it and see." Pulling out one of the chairs, Aidan sank into it with a weary sigh and began to remove the medical tape that held a large bandage to his thigh.

Connor set the blob on the table before following suit and withdrawing a chair for himself. "What happened to your leg?"

"Some whacked-out chick happened to it." The cotton fell away from damaged skin, exposing a puckered pink scar beneath a row of perfect stitches. Aidan's eyes lifted and met Connor's. "She was one of us, I think. She had Elite boots on and," Aidan waved his hand over the pile on the table, "all of this was hers."

"Whacked out, eh?" Connor groaned and ran his hands through his hair, lacing his fingers together at his nape. "As in creepy eyes and a serious need for dental work?"

Aidan stilled. "*That's* why you're here."

"Yep."

"She had razor-sharp teeth and pitch black eyes. No sclera at all. How the hell is that possible?"

"According to the dreams I've been having, she's what happens when the Elders screw up."

"*Dreams?*"

"I know." Connor heaved out his breath. "I don't know if my imagination is smarter than I gave myself credit for or if someone in the Twilight is communicating with me. In any case, I've had two almost-identical dreams. In each one Sheron finds me by the lake and tells me that the Elders tried to replicate the Medium slipstreams from the cavern inside the Temple and Nightmares infiltrated the streams, merging with the Guardians who made the journey, which created those 'whacked-out' things. He called them hybrids."

Growling, Aidan rubbed at the back of his neck. "We need to know if that's true or not."

"No shit." Raising his brows, Connor asked, "You did kill her, right?"

"Right."

"Good. That's one down."

"Fuck." Aidan's hand fisted, wadding up the bandage. "How many are there?"

"Sheron said they sent ten Guardians through the first time and twenty the second time. There's no telling how many of them were infected. Remembering the games he used to play during training at the academy, I'm guessing they sent more than that and he's keeping the real number to himself."

"I agree." Standing, Aidan moved to the kitchen and tossed the waste in the trash. "I need coffee," he muttered. "Lyssa and I haven't slept in two days. I spotted the red-head yesterday afternoon and we've been running nonstop ever since."

"*Red* hair?" Red wasn't a natural color in their species. Pure white . . . various shades of blond and brown . . . hair so black it looked liquid, yes. Any shade of red, impossible.

"Yeah. It's what first caught my eye. Neon red. You couldn't miss it. It threw me off, because no Elite would deliberately draw attention to themselves." Aidan snagged a bag of coffee beans from the freezer and tossed it on the counter. "Now, I'm guessing the Nightmare's need to feed is what drove her to do it. Similar to waving a cape before a bull to bring it close enough to kill."

"*If* we want to put stock in my dreams."

Aidan grimaced. "It might be crazy, but what else have we got to work with?"

Connor watched his friend move around the small galley kitchen with quiet efficiency, pulling mugs from the dishwasher and filling the coffeemaker with water.

"You look happy," he noted. Aidan had a loose-limbed grace and easy smile that hadn't been seen in ages. In fact, that inner contentment had been absent for so long, Connor had forgotten Aidan ever had it.

"I am," Aidan said.

"Do you ever get homesick?"

"All the time."

The ready reply startled Connor. "You don't show it. You look centuries younger." The silver strands that once lined Aidan's temples were far less numerous. They were now barely noticeable unless one was actively searching for them.

"You've been in my head. You know why."

Yes, Connor knew why. Having melded with Aidan's subconscious, he had experienced Aidan's existence in live action and living color. He had felt the way Aidan did when Lyssa was near, felt the emotions she aroused with a single touch or a loving glance, felt the depth of Aidan's hunger when Lyssa made love to him with wild, fervent abandon. Their connection was hauntingly intimate. The few times Connor had met with Aidan in the dream state, it felt like trespassing to share those memories.

"I'm sure you hate it here," Aidan said, looking at him over the breakfast bar, "but I'm glad you came. There's less to be homesick about with you around. Plus, I realize now that I need help and there's no one I trust more than you."

Connor looked away, unsure of how to reply. Aidan was like a brother to him, but he didn't know how to say it. "You know I'm always looking for an opportunity to throw down and kick some ass," he hedged gruffly. "Wager's the go-to-guy when it comes to figuring out the technical aspects of what's going on. I'm the muscle. Always have been. Really don't think I have it in me to be anything more than that."

"I think you underestimate yourself." Aidan smiled with an ease Connor hadn't seen since their academy days. Dressed in knee-length khaki shorts and a bright blue T-shirt, he looked very human. "You're the biggest guy I know and the bravest, but you're also intuitive and . . ."

"Shut up. You're embarrassing me." Aidan's praise warmed Connor in a way very few things could. He admired his best friend and commanding officer, always had. Aidan was born to lead, a solid anchor to grasp in any situation.

"I know. Your face is red."

"Asshole."

Aidan laughed.

Connor quickly changed the subject. "We broke into the Temple and downloaded what we could before I was attacked by one of those Nightmare aberrations."

"Did you get anything useful?" Aidan asked, alert.

"Wager's still digging, but he found out that the Elders-in-training in the tubes are batteries of some sort."

"Batteries? Like a power source?"

"Exactly. The interior of the tubes are filled with energy. That's keeping the guys alive without food and water. The whole time we were thinking something was providing power to the tubes, but it's the reverse. The tubes are providing power for something else. We haven't figured out what yet."

Aidan frowned. "I suppose it's possible. We exist because of cellular energy. The tubes must tap into that."

"That's what Wager said. There are thousands of those tubes, so either they give off very little power—in which case, why use them?—or whatever they're hooked up to requires tremendous amounts of energy."

Aidan stood there, frozen. "How could they have kept all of this hidden for so long?"

"We let them." Connor pushed up from the chair and stretched. "Guardians like me who were too busy wandering aimlessly through life to give a shit. I feel like an idiot. A blind, stubborn idiot."

"You trusted those who swore to protect us. There's nothing to be ashamed of."

"Whatever," Connor scoffed. "I'm a moron. You've got to feel vindicated, though. You were right."

"It's not vindication I feel," Aidan said wearily, holding up an empty mug in silent query. "Pissed off and sick to my stomach is more like it."

Connor shook his head in response to the offer of coffee. "So where do we go from here? Where the hell do we begin?"

"With what we've got." Aidan filled two mugs, preparing one with cream and sweetener before drinking the one he kept black. He left a clean cup by the coffeepot for Stacey and the sight of that lone vessel did something odd to Conner. The urge to know how she liked her coffee took him by surprise. Such a minor detail, barely personal, and yet it mattered to him. He frowned.

"I thought I spotted Elder Rachel at an auction once," Aidan continued, leaning back into the counter edge and holding his green Rainforest Café mega mug with both hands. "I can't be sure since it's been ages since she left the Elite and joined the Elders, but the resemblance was uncanny and I can't think of anyone more likely to *want* to come here."

An image of a raven haired Guardian came to Connor's mind. "I saw that memory when I visited with you in the dream state. We talked about her being an excellent warrior. I think I served with her at the Gateway once. She's a bad-ass chick if I ever saw one. Loves combat."

All Guardians who wished to join the ranks of the Elite were required to spend a month at the Gateway as an initiation to the most extreme rigors of their job. The vast majority of fledglings failed to last the miniscule length of time required. Only a month, a drop in the endless well of time in their lives, but at the Gateway, it felt like an eternity.

Because the Gateway was hell, the place some Dreamers saw when they were on the verge of death and believed was ruled by a red-skinned man with a forked tail and horned head. It was a place all Guardians wished they could ignore and forget, but that was impossible. It was the entryway to the Twilight, an opening the Elders had created in order to give them a place to hide from the Nightmares. But their refuge had been discovered and they were now under constant siege.

The vast door to the Outer Realm bulged with the effort to keep the Nightmares out. Slivers of red light around the jamb revealed how the portal strained at the hinges and lock. From those tiny cracks, black shadows poured in like water and infected the Twilight around the Gateway until lava-spewing pustules formed from the ground. There, thousands of Elite Warriors fought an endless battle, their glaives flashing as they cut down Nightmares in countless numbers. It was an onerous task and one no sane Guardian wished to experience any longer than they were forced to.

Except for Rachel.

She had lasted the month and then argued that she could handle a month more.

"Yes. Kick-ass," Aidan agreed. "Plus, she's got a hefty advantage. She knows what the fuck is going on. I don't. She's got one mission. My focus is divided. I've got to keep Lyssa safe, take care of acquisitions for McDougal, and hunt down the artifacts. And now that we've got those . . . *things* . . . to deal with, there's no way for you and I to do it alone. Two against a widespread group of freaks? I might as well give up, grab Lyssa, and go hide out on a deserted island until everything blows up. Snatch a little peace while I can."

"Shit." Connor blew out his breath. "You're right. We need reinforcements, but hell if I know who'll want to come here. The men under my command are committed to the cause, but . . ."

"But this is asking a lot."

"Yeah. It is. For most of us, the Twilight is the only home we've ever known. There aren't many around who remember the Old World. Asking them to leave everything behind for this," he waved his arm in a sweeping gesture, "is a tall order."

"It sucks, but what choice do we have?" Aidan rubbed one hand across the morning whiskers that shadowed his jaw. "The redhead had the *taza* I was searching for, so they're tracking the artifacts. I need to concentrate on keeping McDougal happy, because he's paying the bills. We need someone to hunt the artifacts while I'm working and a group to hunt the hybrids. The thing that attacked me was insane. One of them is going to get caught or killed and then the Dreamers will know they're not alone in the Universe."

"And anyone close to you is in danger, too, and needs protection. The Elders will use whatever they can for leverage. You think I'd kick Stacey to the curb because of boredom. Fact is, I'd stay away from her because hanging with me could get her killed."

Narrowing his gaze, Aidan studied him carefully.

"Here's the thing, though," Connor continued, too impatient to try explaining feelings he didn't understand. "The roundtrip isn't without its consequences. The Medium is destroyed on the return."

Aidan stilled. "Destroyed?"

"Killed. Murdered. Game over."

"Fuck."

"Pretty much. So it's not as if we can promise a temporary assignment."

There was a long pause, then, "Thank you."

The two words were spoken with such feeling that Connor was taken aback. "For what?"

"For giving up your home for me. Shit . . . "

Aidan's eyes reddened and Connor panicked. "Hey! Don't get excited, man. It's okay."

"No. It's not. It's awesome. I don't know what to say."

"Don't say anything," Conner said hastily.

Lyssa entered from the living room and Connor almost kissed her with relief. "Umm . . . Coffee," she crooned. She sported a damp ponytail, clean clothes, and smelled like apples. Dressed in a dark pink velour jogging suit, she looked revived and beautiful. She found the cup Aidan had prepared for her and lifted to her tiptoes to kiss him full on the mouth. "Thank you, baby," she whispered.

Connor, grateful for the opportunity, slipped away to change and get ready for the monumental task ahead.

Chapter 8

For a man once lauded for his honor, Michael Sheron's present life filled with lies and treason was an end even he could not have foreseen. The shadowy beings they called Nightmares were nothing compared to the nightmare of deceit he dealt with daily.

As his body flew through air across the distance between the rebellion headquarters and the Temple of the Elders, Michael surveyed the beauty of the landscape rushing by beneath him. Rolling, grass-covered hills. Lush valleys with roaring rivers. Magnificent waterfalls.

All a carefully crafted stage to stave off discontent.

It saddened him that he had come to disdain the paradise he expended great effort to maintain, but the perfection of their surroundings was as evanescent as the dreams his people guarded. Beneath the façade lay a foundation firmly mired in untruths. But only the Elders and the rebels knew this. The majority of Guardians were happy here and they would remain that way, *if* they were kept ignorant of the uprising.

That deception was his most pressing task, and it grew more difficult by the day. Captain Aidan Cross was a warrior of legend, his mere presence enough to make the other Guardians feel safe and secure. Cross's disappearance was beginning to cause undue speculation and now the loss of Bruce would compound the problem.

They were the two most visible and acclaimed members of the Elite Warriors and lifelong best friends. The Guardians wouldn't understand why two men so fiercely loyal to their people would betray them so brutally. Their desertion would raise questions regarding what had so disillusioned them, and the option—to make them villains—was not one Michael wanted to utilize. He thought it best to keep both men in the good graces of the masses. Hero worship was a powerful emotion, and it could be a useful tool in the future. History was filled with tales of great feats accomplished by invoking the memory of a beloved figure.

The gleaming white Temple came into view and Michael slowed his airborne glide, drifting into a vertical position and then lowering gently to his feet. He paused a moment to pull up the cowl all the Elders used to hide their emaciated features from public view. He'd once been a handsome man. Ages ago. The loss of physical beauty, however, was a small price to pay to achieve his aims.

Outwardly prepared, Michael stepped through the massive red *torii* gate the Elders used as a motivator. Its warning engraved in the ancient language—*Beware of the Key that turns the Lock*—had given the Guardians both a goal and hope, two things required to maintain mental health. If he could keep the knowledge of the coup contained, the message could continue to serve its purpose.

As he crossed the open-air center courtyard, he left a trail of droplets in his wake. His robes were still soaked from his confrontation with Bruce and would have to remain that way for the time being. He was expected, and punctuality was the best way to stave off unwanted curiosity.

Knowing he was being watched through the vid monitors, Michael kept his movements to a leisurely pace. He paused at the *chôzuya*. Dipping the waiting ladle into the fountain, he rinsed out his mouth and washed his hands, his gaze sweeping over his surroundings, a place that brought comfort to most Guardians but felt like a prison to him.

Releasing his breath, he cleared his mind, knowing that a confident and casually arrogant mien would be required to get him through the audience ahead. He had suggested meeting with Bruce, but the events he had set in motion during that discussion were entirely of his own design. It was a complicated dance he engaged in, and a misstep would cost him everything.

Michael traversed the courtyard and entered the *haiden* where the other Elders awaited him. His peers. Or so they called themselves. In truth, there were very few of the many who shared his goals.

The cool interior engulfed him, the room's rounded walls hidden in shadow due to the light that illuminated only the dead center of the space. He came to a halt within that beam and it immediately dimmed, revealing the hooded figures who sat before him in semicircular rows.

"Has Captain Bruce connected with Cross and the Key, Elder Sheron?"

"If he has not done so yet, he will shortly."

The benches above him exploded in a hum of dozens of conversations. Michael waited patiently, his stance wide, his hands clasped at the small of his back. With a toss of his head, his wet cowl was thrown back to better convince the others of his sincerity. No one feigned sincerity as well as he did.

"What do you suggest we do now that Bruce is out of the Twilight?"

"We should send an Elder to lead the team recovering the artifacts."

Discussion swelled again, hundreds of voices competing to be heard over the din.

"Sheron."

He smiled inwardly at the feminine voice. "Yes, Elder Rachel?"

"Who would you send on our behalf?"

"Who would you prefer?"

Rachel stood, pushing her hood back to reveal raven tresses and snapping green eyes. "I will go. And lead."

"You were exactly who I had in mind," he drawled.

Elder Rachel was a warrior of singular skill who had a rare gift for command, much like Cross and Bruce. Her appearance was also a plus. Only the female Elders retained their youthful attractiveness. She would not be as conspicuous as the men would be.

"Captain Cross will have difficulty facing a woman opponent," he said. "That is an advantage we will need."

"And Bruce?" someone questioned. "I still do not understand how his presence in the mortal realm helps us in any way."

"Each of them is immovable alone. Together, they are fluid. They lean on each other. They have more to lose when they know their actions affect the other one. They will become more firmly rooted in the mortal plane. They will venture farther, experience more, take bigger risks than they would have apart."

"It will take too long!" someone complained.

Michael sighed inwardly. "If we hope to have the Dreamer conceive a Guardian sired child, we will need to give them time. They are poised on a knife's edge and until they feel secure enough in their future together, they won't chance pregnancy. Regardless, the gestational period for a human female cannot be changed."

"But she is not like other humans."

"Which creates even more questions," he argued. "We cannot rush this. We must be patient and allow the pieces of the puzzle to fall where they may."

Discussion ensued and lasted for hours. It was always this way. The Guardian community was resistant to change by nature. Michael often thought it was a fortuitous circumstance that they were immortal. Otherwise, they would never have the lifespan required to accomplish any task.

In the end, however, he achieved his aims.

"Elder Rachel, you will begin preparations?" an Elder asked. "The acclimation to the human world will not be easy and working against Captain Cross will test you."

Her lush mouth curved, but the smile wasn't reflected in her hard green eyes. "I will be ready."

"It is decided then," the Elder said, speaking for the collective. "We will proceed to the next chapter."

*   *   *

Stacey finished packing up her stuff and took one last look around Lyssa's guest bedroom to make sure she didn't forget anything.

It was going to suck going home to an empty house, but there was no reason to stay and she really didn't want to. The vibe would be too weird now that Lyssa and Aidan knew she'd been intimate with Connor. Besides, Connor was here on business. Knowing how singularly focused Aidan was about his antiquities, they'd probably want to get started right away. She had things to do, too, so . . .

Slinging one strap of her backpack over her shoulder, Stacey headed downstairs.

She was surprised to find Connor alone. He was seated at the dining table, gingerly cleaning some dirt-encrusted object. A black T-shirt stretched to its limits over his broad shoulders and his long legs were encased in loose-fitting faded jeans.

"Hi," she said, as she passed him on her way to fetching her purse from the top of the breakfast bar. "Where's Aidan and Lyssa?"

"They went to sleep. Apparently, they drove all night and they're wiped out."

Stacey turned to face him. He watched her with those aqua eyes that seemed so knowing. As if he'd seen and done more than was possible for a man of his years. He couldn't be more than thirty-five, she'd guess, but he had the stamina and energy of a man half that age, as she knew firsthand.

She shook her head. "I was hoping they'd enjoy some time off. They both work too damn hard."

"Where are you going?" he asked softly, his eyes on her baby pink and black Roxy backpack. She would never have purchased such an extravagance for herself. A five dollar backpack from Wal-Mart would do the same job. But Lyssa had noted her admiring it in the store and bought it as a gift. Because of that, it was one of her favorite "luxury" items.

"Home. I have some things to do."

"Like what?"

"Stuff. The house needs cleaning. I can rarely get to it when Justin's home. And the front step on my porch is rotted. My neighbor said he'd take a look at it for me, so I'll see if today works for him or not."

Connor set the object in his hands down and pushed back from the table in a dangerously graceful movement. For as big as he was, he moved like a panther. Sleek and stealthy. "I can fix it for you."

She blinked up at him, her head tilted back slightly to take in his height. Even from a few feet away, she had to raise her eye level to look at him. "Why?"

"Why would he fix it for you?" he countered.

Stacey frowned. "Because he's a nice guy."

"I'm a nice guy."

"You're busy." And gorgeous. Dear god, he was luscious. Black was his color, for sure. She'd noted that yesterday when he arrived. It accentuated his golden skin and hair to perfection. The slightly too-long locks, T-shirt, jeans, and black combat boots made a heady bad boy combination. The mental picture of him in her house did strange things to her equilibrium.

"I need to strategize," he said. "I can do that anywhere."

"Fixing a broken step is boring."

"Your neighbor doesn't think so."

"He likes my homemade apple pie."

Connor crossed his arms over his chest. "I like apple pie."

"It's really not a good idea . . ."

"Sure it is," he insisted, with a stubborn bent to his jaw line that she found endearing. "I'm great at fixing porches."

She should say no. Really. She knew he was hoping that a quick repair would lead to some sexual gratitude. Thing of it was, she was worried he might be right to hope. She'd spent the entire length of her shower wondering what it would be like to make love to him with time on her side. Without rushing through it.

Hazardous thoughts.

"I think we should just say good-bye now," she said.

"Chicken."

Her mouth fell open. "Excuse me?"

Connor tucked his hands in his arm pits, flapped his arms up and down, and made squawking noises.

"Oh my god," she muttered. "That's so childish."

"Whatever. You're scared to take me with you because you like me too much."

"I do not."

"Liar."

She set her hands on her hips and asked, "Why do all men regress to being big babies when they don't get what they want?"

He stuck his tongue out at her.

Stacey bit her lower lip and looked away quickly. He

laughed, a full-bodied guffaw of pure joy. She choked while trying to keep from joining him.

"Come on. Enough of this nonsense." He rounded the dining table and took her backpack from her. The grin he gifted her with made her tummy flip. "I promise to behave."

"But I'm so irresistible," she drawled wryly.

"I know."

The intimate timbre to his brogue arrested her and kept her staring at him long after she should have looked away. His gaze was warm and possessive, slightly hungry. She was asking for trouble with a capital "T" by taking him home with her. Letting him play man of the house for the afternoon. Allowing him to imprint himself on her home.

She sighed. "What if *I* don't behave?"

Connor stepped aside and gestured toward the foyer. "I won't say no," he warned. "If you're hoping I'll agree to play the gentleman, think again."

"Fine." Stacey led the way to the front door and he opened it, pausing a moment to collect his sword. "But I'm putting you to work, Mr. Big-strong-man-who-can-do-the-chicken-dance."

"Bring it on, sweetheart."

He followed her out the white wooden gate that enclosed Lyssa's flagstone patio. They walked together to the small guest parking area and Stacey hit the remote on her keychain that popped open the trunk of her Nissan Sentra. Connor tossed her backpack and his scabbard inside, then began whistling as he moved to the passenger door.

"You're too happy about this," she muttered.

"And you're too worried." He paused and stared at her

over the roof of her car. "We had sex, Stacey. Great sex." His voice lowered and the brogue thickened. "I've been *inside* you. If I can't be happy spending time with you after that, what kind of guy would that make me?"

Stacey swallowed hard, blinking. She'd seen this look on his face before. Austerely intent. Serious. He wore it just as well as he wore amusement. "You're fucking with my head. I don't like it."

"By telling you the truth?"

"By being perfect!" she hissed, glancing around to make sure they weren't being overheard. "Stop it."

His mouth curved in a tender smile. "You're nuts, you know that?"

"Yeah?" She yanked open her car door and slid behind the wheel. "You don't have to hang out with me."

The passenger door opened and he folded his big body into the suddenly miniscule seat. He grimaced.

"Move the seat back if you won't go away," she said.

He shook his head and looked exasperated. "I'm not going anywhere. Get used to the idea."

Rolling her eyes, Stacey leaned over and reached between his legs to find the manual seat release. "Don't think you're going to make me feel guilty that you're squished. Push back."

He didn't move.

"Jesus H. Christ!" She smacked his shin. "Why are you so stubborn? Push back."

He still didn't move. Not one muscle.

Turning her head to complain, she found herself eye level with an impressive bulge in the crotch of his jeans. His right hand was on his thigh, the fingers white as they dug into the hard muscle beneath the denim. Stunned for a moment, Stacey didn't move. Comprehension was slow to sink in. Eventually she realized that her breasts were pressed to his left thigh, thrusting rhythmically due to her labored breathing. Her gaze lifted, noting the rapid lift and fall of his chest before coming to rest on his face.

His expression was mocking. "This is supposed to make me more comfortable?"

Stacey glared and straightened. "You did that on purpose."

Connor snorted and moved the seat back himself. "Let's go, sweetheart."

They pulled out of Lyssa's gated condominium complex and sped down the road to Stacey's part of town. Old town, they called it, but it was presently going through an overhaul. The new police station and town hall were being built in one large complex, and new businesses were filling the once empty plots. Murrieta was a new town with an old history. Within a block of each other, one could find a Starbucks and a farm. The dichotomy was one she relished. Country charm with all the modern conveniences.

"Do you like it here?" Connor asked, surveying the passing landscape with a curious eye.

"I do. It's perfect for me."

"What do you like about it?"

She glanced aside at him. "What's not to like?"

He wrinkled his nose. "It stinks."

"O-kay . . ." Stacey pondered that a moment. "We *are* in a valley." At his raised brows, she explained, "Smog tends to sit in valleys."

"Wonderful."

She shrugged. "If you think it stinks here, don't go to Norco."

"Sounds like a gas station," he said.

She laughed. "I've always thought so, too! Seriously, though, it's horse country. Plus they have lots of dairy farms out that way. The whole town smells like cow shit."

"Nice." His mouth was curved in that singular smile that made her heart flutter madly.

They turned a corner and entered the part of old Murrieta where there were no sidewalks and there was a good bit of distance between one house and the next. It was far different from the area where Lyssa lived. There you could borrow a cup of sugar from a neighbor just by reaching your arm out your window.

Stacey pulled into her gravel drive and came to a stop before the little two-bedroom house she called home. It was small, just under a thousand square feet, but it was adorable. If she said so herself. It had a wide covered front porch framed by curving flower beds that she'd designed and planted herself. Painted a soft sage green with bright white trim, the place was cute on the outside and fully modernized on the inside. And it was hers.

Well, as much as a mortgaged house could be.

"Here it is," she said, lifting her chin with pride.

Connor rounded the trunk and drew abreast of her. "I like it."

She glanced at him and found him engrossed in checking out her abode. "It's too small for you," she thought aloud, then instantly regretted how that might come across. As if she were imagining him living there.

He canted his body to face her, standing so close she

couldn't help but smell him. She didn't know what the scent was. It wasn't any cologne that she could recognize. It was just him, she suspected. *Just Connor*—brilliant name for a signature cologne and he'd make a fortune off it.

"I like tight places," he purred with mischief in his eyes.

Not for the first time, Stacey wondered what it would be like to live with a man who was so confident. That inner surety enabled him to be such a shameless tease. It also made him different from all the other men she had ever dated. The others had been small men pretending to be big men. She'd always fallen for the shell, the illusion of stability. Until she had Justin. Then she learned to find strength within herself, because someone else depended on her.

She inched by Connor and went to the trunk where she pulled out her backpack. Evading him when he tried to take it from her, Stacey jogged to the porch and cautioned, "Watch out for the second stair. That's the one with the rot."

"Got it."

When she pulled open the wooden-framed screen door, he was right there with her, his hand catching the edge and holding it ajar while she unlocked the two deadbolts and door lock.

"Isn't it safe out here?" he asked, delaying entering the house after her because he was scanning the front yard and the quiet street beyond.

"Yes. But my scaredy-cat sensibilities take over after dark."

He nodded as if he understood. Stacey suspected he sympathized, but she doubted he had ever been scared of anything. He was too steady, too assured. She imagined that resoluteness came from growing up in a family so dedicated to dangerous military service. They all expected to die, so they didn't fear danger in the same way others did.

He stepped into her living room behind her and the screen door swung shut with a loud squeak followed by a louder bang. Connor scowled at it. "Your door's broken."

"Technically, it's the little arm thingy that doesn't work, not the door."

"Whatever. It's busted."

"Nah, it needs adjustment. Make yourself comfortable." Stacey headed down the hallway to the laundry room, where she pulled her cat hair-covered clothes out of her backpack and tossed them in the washing machine.

A moment later Connor called after her, "Your son is a handsome boy."

Stacey blew out her breath and headed back toward the living room. Connor was half-way down the hall, looking at the multitude of framed pictures that lined the length. It was a small space and he hogged all of it, the top of his head nearly reaching the low ceiling.

"Thanks. I think so." She found him studying a Polaroid of the two of them at the Cub Scout Pinewood Derby. Justin had been nearly of a height with her, and with his medium brown hair and dark eyes he didn't really look related to her at all.

"That was taken a couple years ago," she explained. "He's dropped out of Cub Scouts since then. Said it was something a boy should do with his dad."

Connor reached over and stroked his hand down the

length of her spine. It was a gesture of comfort, much like the kiss he'd given her the night before, and it *was* a source of consolation, but it was something else, too. And she couldn't let it be something else. She couldn't allow him to become a crutch she looked toward or depended on, because he wasn't going to be around forever.

She'd made the same mistake so many times—looking for strength outside of herself. She refused to do it again.

"I'll go start on the pie," she said before passing him and heading into the kitchen. It took him a while to join her, and when he did he wore an odd expression.

"You alright?" she asked, turning off the water she had running to wash the apples. "All the family stuff freaking you out? Want me to take you home?"

"Aidan's house isn't home." He leaned against the jamb of the archway that connected the breakfast nook with the kitchen. There was no formal dining room, which worked because she didn't need one.

He watched her intently, a brooding and overwhelming presence in her tiny kitchen. "Am I supposed to freak out because you have a child?"

His arms crossed his chest in a now familiar gesture, emphasizing his mouthwatering biceps. He dominated her thoughts, making it impossible to avoid being highly aware of him. A larger-than-life personality housed in a larger-than-life body. It was too much. *He* was too much.

"I don't know." She shook out the excess water from the colander. "You came in here looking funny."

"It's been a rough couple days."

"Wanna talk about it?"

"I do, actually."

"Okay. Shoot." She dug into one of the lower cabinets for her apple peeler.

"I can't."

Stacey straightened and hid her unreasonable feeling of hurt and disappointment with a caustic, "Of course not."

"You wouldn't believe me."

"I'll have to take your word for it." She met his gaze and held it. "Since I've got nothing else to go on."

They both waited a long moment. She sensed the conflict in him, the need to say something important, but she couldn't figure out what it would be.

So she made her best guess. "You're not going to be living in the Valley full-time, are you?"

He frowned. "I have to travel a lot."

"Okay." She sighed. "You're not going to ask me to be exclusive when you're in town, but single when you're not, right? Please don't."

"I'm not an asshole, Stacey," he said with quiet dignity. "Can you raise the bar a little when you think about me?"

Connor watched Stacey fidget nervously and inwardly kicked himself. He was bungling this all to hell, but he didn't know how to fix it.

He wanted to be with her.

It was as simple and as complicated as that.

She sighed audibly. "I'm sorry." She tossed her hands up. "I just don't know what you're doing here. Why you're looking at me like that. What I'm supposed to do or say."

I'm here because I couldn't let you go home alone when there are freaks out there. I'm looking at you like this because I've been in your room and I touched the blankets on your bed that keep you warm. I want you to say that you want me there. With you.

With an impatient hand, she pushed the mass of dark curls back from her face. He knew she wanted promises and stability. Perhaps not promises of forever, but he couldn't even guarantee her anything beyond this moment. He might be on a plane tonight with no clue when he would be back. The best way to keep her safe was by stopping the danger before it reached her.

Aidan was right. Connor knew he was the worst possible choice for her, but that didn't silence the part of him that insisted she was his to take care of.

He straightened. "Do you have tools?"

Busy work. That's what he needed. Something to occupy him physically while his brain worked to sort out his dilemma. Otherwise, he'd be all over her in a minute, coaxing and seducing her into the tumble he so desperately wanted. Face to face. Her legs wrapped around his hips. Her nails in his back.

"Only the basics." Her green eyes gave so much away. He wondered if she knew that. "They're in a yellow metal bucket just inside the door."

"I'll get to work."

"Thank you."

Gratitude. He heard it in her voice and the primitive part of his psyche wanted to howl in victory. She needed something and he could provide it.

Mine.

Connor had never felt even the slightest bit possessive about a lover in his life. But then he hadn't felt even the slightest bit like himself since he'd met Stacey.

He caught up the bucket handle, pushed open the screen door, and stepped out onto the porch. There was a good bit of distance from the house to the street. A wide expanse of lawn took over from the flower beds and ran all the way to the chain link fence.

It was a cute house. Quaint and charming. It was a home that suited Stacey and revealed another side of her. He wanted to stay for dinner and another movie. He wanted to love her body again, the right way. The long way. All night. He wanted to wake up with her wiggling her delightful ass against his cock. Only this time they'd both be naked. He could anchor her leg on his hip and push into her from behind—

The door slammed shut behind him.

"That's got to go," he growled, turning to glare at the offending object.

Connor set down the tools and got to work. He forcibly pushed thoughts of Elders and Nightmares from his mind. He had only this single day with Stacey and though he'd come here because he feared for her traveling alone, he now intended to spend the hours with her indulging as if there were no tomorrow.

Because, for them, there wasn't.

 Chapter 9

"There!"

Pushing to his feet, Connor stood on the now repaired step and jumped up and down. It bore the abuse beautifully.

"Yum," Stacey purred.

Glancing up as the screen door opened, he watched her step outside. "Hi."

"Hi back."

Connor knew that look she had in her eyes. Other women had been giving it to him for ages. It was the first time he'd gotten it from Stacey, though, and coupled with the unconscious licking of her lips it heated his blood.

"Sweetheart," he purred, "you look ready to eat me alive."

"Have you been out here shirtless the whole time?" she asked, a bit breathlessly. She'd put her hair up into adorable pigtails and was carrying two glasses filled with reddish liquid on ice. For some reason, the girlish hairstyle made him hot as hell. There was nothing immature about

Stacey, but the look brought to mind some role-playing that he'd love to indulge in with her.

"The last half hour or so."

"I'm sorry I missed it."

His mouth curved. "I'm still here."

She looked as if she was considering his offer. He helped her along a little by reaching down and stoking the straining length of his erection through his jeans.

"Christ, you're brazen," she muttered, eyes riveted.

"You want me. I want you back," he said simply. "My body gets ready to follow through. Pointless to pretend otherwise."

Stacey blew out her breath and then smiled with false cheerfulness. It didn't reach her eyes, which were clouded with confusion and longing. "I thought you might enjoy some cranberry juice."

He knew when to push and when to pull back.

"I'd love some." The food tasted better here; he'd give the mortal plane that much credit. The Chinese food had been phenomenal, as was the glass of orange juice he had enjoyed in lieu of coffee that morning. He could picture a life of overeating and then burning off all the extra energy in bed with Stacey.

Paradise. A dream.

"Hey!" he said with exaggerated mock surprise. He lifted a hand to his ear. "Hear that?"

She froze on the third step with a frown marring the space between her brows. Then her eyes widened. Tossing a quick glance over her shoulder at the porch, she cried, "You fixed the door!" Her delighted smile hit him hard, because this time it lit up her beautiful green eyes.

He shrugged as if he weren't all puffed up with manly pride. "Technically, it was the little arm thingy that didn't work."

Stacey came down the last few steps and handed him a glass. She caught one his fingers with a quick scissor of her own and held him in place. "Thank you."

"You're very welcome." Connor stood there a moment, forcing himself to breathe in measured rhythm.

She looked away. Releasing him, she walked over to the porch railing and rested her elbows atop it. She seemed melancholy and he didn't know what to say, so he sank into the nearby swinging bench and drank deeply.

"With your family so dedicated to military service," she began, "why did you retire? Were you injured?"

Connor inhaled sharply, debating how to reply. In the end, he found that he could only be truthful with her. "I lost faith in our government," he admitted, watching carefully for her reaction. "When I no longer believed they were acting in the best interests of the people, I had to leave."

"Oh." She looked at him with sympathy. "I'm sorry. You sound so disappointed."

And she sounded as if she cared that he was, which hit him like a heat wave, misting his skin with sweat. The only person he shared anything personal with was Aidan and the comfort Connor received from him was entirely different from the comfort Stacey provided. She made him want to share more, give her more of himself, increase their bond because it strengthened him to know she was there.

"I *wanted* to trust them." He rocked gently, enjoying the afternoon breeze that smelled like freshly cut grass and the fragrant flowers Stacey had planted around the porch. He wasn't home, but he felt as if he was. "It's tough realizing that you deliberately fooled yourself because the truth was too painful to acknowledge."

"Connor." She sighed and came toward him. He slid over to give her room to sit next to him.

"So where do you go from here?" she asked, staring into the contents of her glass.

"I don't know. Once Aidan recovers, we'll sit down and figure out what's next."

"Are you working for McDougal, too?"

"No."

"How long will you be here?"

"I don't know. Not long. Another day, maybe."

"Oh . . ."

They rocked together in silence for a time and he watched her from beneath heavy-lidded eyes, noting her restlessly moving fingers. She'd changed into a pink tank top and overall shorts that bared her lithe legs. He was enamored with the view, riveted by the flex and release of her thigh muscles as she pushed the swing to and fro.

"I bet you're excited to go."

His mouth curved ruefully. "Why do you say that?"

Stacey gestured around them with a wide sweep of her hand. "You must be bored."

"Must I?" Connor reached over, wrapped his arm around her slim waist and tugged her closer. "What would you be doing if I wasn't here?"

She shrugged. "Cleaning. Laundry. Sometimes I run over to the Movie Experience and catch the latest action flick."

"Don't you date?" he asked softly.

"I rarely have time." She glanced furtively at him. "There also aren't a lot of men interested in single mothers."

"That's not all you are." His fingers slid up her side to where her tank top was bared by the arm opening of her overalls. He stroked the side of her breast and felt the shiver that moved through her. "You're also a woman."

"Something has to take the backseat."

"Sure," he murmured. "But you're ignoring her completely."

Her chin lifted. "Not everyone has the ability to have casual sex."

"I agree."

Stacey canted her torso away from his touch, which brought her almost face to face with him. "How do *you* do it?"

His nostrils flared. "Why do you want to know?"

"Maybe I can use some pointers."

"Sweetheart." He yanked and pulled her chest flush to his. Her drink sloshed over the lip of her glass and splashed on the porch, but neither of them cared. She gasped, her parted lips just an inch or so away from his mouth. "I wouldn't teach you how to have casual sex if you paid me."

The mere thought of another man touching her made him edgy and fierce. His teeth ground together and his fingers kneaded restlessly into her flesh.

Misunderstanding the dangerous possessiveness that affected him, her tongue darted out to lick her bottom lip. He grew hard against her hip and her lashes lowered.

"But then I could have casual sex with you," she flirted.

Connor stared at her a moment in surprise, then he growled. "I don't want to have casual sex with you."

"You don't?"

He shook his head and reached over to set his glass on the small wrought iron table which sat just outside the arc of the swing. Then he cupped her spine with both hands and rubbed just to hear her moan. "I'm not looking forward to leaving. I'm going to regret not enjoying you the way I should have. I'll be kicking myself for a long time for not having any control when I needed it."

"I like that you were wild." She blushed and lowered her gaze to where her hand touched his chest.

"You'd like me better in control," he purred, taking Stacey's glass from her and placing it beside his own. He turned her to face away from him and arranged them comfortably with her back to his chest. Wrapping his arms around her waist, he set his chin atop her head and pushed off, swinging them.

"I could get used to this," he rumbled, closing his eyes and relishing the heated weight of her sweetly curved body against him. His hands slipped beneath the overalls and cupped the firm, full swell of her breasts.

Mine.

But in order to keep her alive, he'd have to let her go.

"I need to go check on the pie," she said weakly, but she made very little effort to extricate herself.

Connor frowned. "I don't know how to get past this."

"Get past what?" She struggled then, and he released her reluctantly.

"Get past your shell."

"My *what?*" Standing, she backed away.

"You're like one of those scaly things that walk really slow and hide inside a round shell."

"A *turtle?*"

"Yep," he nodded gravely, "that's the one. A *snapping* turtle."

The look of outrage on her face was comical, but he refused to smile. They did't have time to skirt around the truth.

"Listen." She set her fists on her hips, her chest heaving with her agitation. "It's not fair to ask me to have noncasual sex with you when you're leaving."

"I know."

"So stop it!"

"I can't," he said simply. "I want you so badly, I ache with it."

She glared at him a moment, then stalked to the door and stormed into the house. Connor cursed under his breath and straightened to a seated position. This was ridiculous. He needed to get out of here and get his head on straight. There was too much that needed to be done and he was only complicating matters by pursuing an attraction that defied logic.

He needed nothing that tied him down and held him back; he had to go by necessity. She needed a man to stand by her, support her, take care of her.

Pushing to his feet, Connor moved to the door. He'd call a cab to take him back to Aidan's and then work until they woke up. In a day or two, he'd be far away from here. He just had to stay away from Stacey that long.

As soon as he stepped into the house, the scent of cinnamon, butter, and apples hit him hard enough to bring him up short. He paused just inside the threshold and raking the tiny living room with a sweeping gaze.

The walls were painted ultra-pale yellow, the couch and oversized chair covered in blue-and-white stripes, the coffee and end tables scratched and dented in a way that made a visitor comfortable and relaxed. It was homey and inviting, which was far removed from his starkly furnished bachelor quarters in the Twilight. He'd rarely spent time at home alone, preferring to hang out at Aidan's.

He wanted to spend time here. With Stacey.

Connor tightened his jaw and sat on the couch. He caught up the phone handset from its cradle, reached into the white wicker basket under the table where the yellow pages were stored, and started flipping through the listings. He sensed the moment Stacey walked into the room and glanced up at her. "I'll get out of your—"

He halted mid-sentence, gaping. The pigtails were gone. The shoes were gone. With her fingers at the metal clasp of her overall straps he knew those were about to be gone, too.

"Oh, hell no," she said grimly, reaching into a pocket and tossing a string of condoms at his chest, "you're not getting out of this now."

As he caught the foil strip, every muscle in his body tensed to the point of pain. Coupled with the sight of the overalls falling to the floor—revealing shapely legs and a tiny red lace thong that hardened his dick immediately . . . he groaned.

Control? He'd thought he would have control if they made love again? Was he insane?

"What are you doing, sweetheart?" he asked gruffly.

She arched a brow, grabbed the hem of her tank top,

and yanked it over her head. Her beautiful tits bounced with the violence of her movements. They were the most gorgeous breasts he had ever seen. Pale and tipped with long, rosy nipples. His desire to suck on them flooded his mouth with moisture and he swallowed hard.

"I'm getting naked so I can fuck you," she snapped.

This time, the sound that left him was choked off by the carnal hunger that had him by the balls, fisted tight.

He watched in an agony of lust as her slender fingers hooked beneath the waistband of her panties and pushed them down, revealing a neatly trimmed triangle of black curls. He couldn't move, refused to blink, awed by the sight of her. Short, plump where it counted to ensure he didn't break her when he rode her, with flashing green eyes that burned with passion. Of course, half that passion was anger, but he could fix that, if he could get his brain to work.

Stacey stalked toward him, gloriously vibrant. He knew he was in trouble. His stomach was knotted up and his breathing erratic. Even when facing a legion of Nightmares, he was never like this. It was as if every step she took toward him was a step forward that couldn't be backtracked. He was both excited and scared shitless.

Then she was crawling over him, straddling his lap, and every labored inhale he took was filled with her scent. Lush, willing, aroused woman. Unlike any other woman in his history.

The slight tinge of fear he'd felt melted into a feeling of rightness he could not deny. He didn't feel trapped by Stacey's longing. He craved it, craved her, and only when she was in his arms did the gnawing ease.

She reached for the button and zipper of his jeans and the feel of her fingers brushing along the length of his cock snapped him out of his daze. He reached between her legs, parting her with his fingers, finding her slick and hot.

"Yes," she breathed, tugging harder at the button of his jeans, which was difficult to free because he was sitting.

"Let me eat you," he said gruffly, desperate for the taste of her on his tongue.

Tension stiffened her frame and she stared at his mouth with heavy-lidded eyes. He bit his lower lip, then released it slowly, feeling her quiver beneath his stroking fingertips. Circling her clit, he licked his lips. She whimpered and her nipples stiffened further, directly before his face.

Leaning forward, he opened his mouth and sucked her in. It wasn't enough, not nearly. He cupped the other breast with his free hand, squeezing and kneading, feeling it swell and grow heavy with her desire. Cheeks hollowing, he pressed a puffy nipple to the roof of his mouth and licked his tongue back and forth along the underside of it. Rubbing between her legs, relishing the sounds she made, the mewls and gasps, the way she writhed against him and dug her nails into the bare skin of his shoulders.

He stroked two fingers over the slitted entrance to her pussy, then pushed inside her. She was soaked, dripping down his fingers, clenching greedily as he began to fuck her. In and out. Working her cunt with every bit of skill he possessed, making her cream and beg for his cock.

"Please . . . fuck me . . ."

He loved it. Would never get enough of it. Not for his ego, but for her. Because he wanted her to be happy. He wanted to be the man capable of making her happy.

"Connor . . . please . . . !"

All the while he suckled her, nibbling with lips and teeth, flicking rapidly over the hard peak with his tongue. She began to grind her hips, fucking him back, lifting and falling, riding his plunging fingers. Her cunt was so drenched he could hear it as well as feel it, the wet sounds so erotic he feared he would lose it and blow in his pants.

He withdrew his fingers with a growl and released her breast with a wet popping sound. "I need to eat your pussy."

Unable to wait for her help, Connor caught her by the waist, twisted his body, and lay on his back lengthwise along the couch. She cried out in surprise as he pulled her up and over his mouth, then moaned his name as he lifted his head and licked her from cunt to clit in one heated swipe.

His dick hardened further at the taste of her, making Connor's jeans painfully tight. Connor reached down and freed himself, hissing with relief as the pressure lessened and the open air cooled him enough to take him down a notch.

"Lower," he rasped, tugging her thighs.

Stacey blinked at the golden god sprawled between her obscenely widespread legs and felt the slickness of her lust coating her inner thighs. She'd never been so aroused. He was all over her. Devouring her. Just as she had suspected he would be.

There she'd been, pulling the finished pie out of the oven, imagining what it would be like if they were dating. Imagining what it would be like if this were the beginning and not the end. From the way he was always touching her and teasing her, she guessed he would be the kind of man who would fuck her on the kitchen table because he couldn't wait to get to the bedroom. She pictured him coming up behind her while she worked at the sink, pushing down her shorts, then pushing his cock into her.

He was a primitive, highly sexual male. And she wanted him. Never in all of her years had she met a man such as him. What if she never did again? Balls-to-the-wall sex. Nothing-held-back sex. No-holds-barred sex. She'd only had sex like that once in her life. Last night. With Connor. And it had been phenomenal. Would she be kicking herself later for not enjoying more when she had the chance?

In that moment, with a bubbling apple pie in her gloved hands, Stacey had decided that she was a big girl and she could take it. There were worse things in the world than having a two-night stand with a guy you liked and who liked you back.

"Come down," he repeated, pulling at her, his lips parted and glistening, his gaze dark and hungry. "Sit on my face so I can fuck my tongue deep into you."

Stacey shuddered violently. He was the type of man who enjoyed going down on a woman. Would enjoy driving her crazy and owning her in such a highly personal way. Branding her, making her his.

Today, she wanted to be his.

Clutching the back of the sofa for balance, she came down, biting back the sounds that would have escaped as his hot breath gusted across her wet skin.

"Yes," he purred, his large hands holding the cheeks of her ass and urging her into him. He started licking her, long slow licks, dipping into each groove and crevice, breathing harshly against her. He teased her clit, fluttering feather-light and hummingbird-quick across it.

"Right there," she whispered, rocking into the maddening motion. A firm lick would set her off and she tried to catch it, swiveling her hips, chasing his tongue. Knowing damn well what she needed, Connor moved away from the tiny protrusion, tilted his head, and thrust into her.

"Ah, god!" She was shaking, her fingers white with the strain of gripping the couch back.

Connor growled and pulled her closer, holding her hips and grinding her pussy into his mouth, his tongue fucking fast and deep. Seductive sucking noises filled the air as he drank her down with rough, hungry groans.

The resulting orgasm was devastating, her eyes squeezing shut, her teeth grinding together. Her silence seemed to incite his ardor further. He lifted her and rolled to the side, setting her bottom on the wooden coffee table before looming over her. His lips at her ear, his left hand at her hip, his right dipping between them to position himself at her opening. He lunged hard and deep, pinning her to the surface with the burning length of his thick cock.

She cried out in startled pleasure, her breath caught and held as he thrust one hand into her hair and pulled her head back. He mantled her with his big, hard body. Dominated her. Owned her inside and out. Even his breath was hers. She couldn't breathe without inhaling his exhale.

"Mine," he rumbled, his hand at her hip pulling her hard into him, until there was nothing separating them. He flexed powerfully inside her, as if to say, *I am in you. A part of you.*

The sensation caught the tail end of her orgasm and

caused her to clench tighter around him, reigniting the fading convulsions of her climax.

He groaned as she rippled up and down the length of his cock, his sweat-slick forehead pressing tightly to hers. "You were made for me."

The fit was perfect, if a little snug. Prior to meeting Connor she could have sworn she couldn't take a cock that big. But he made her so damn hot and wet. She rotated her hips in a tentative circle, just to get the full effect of his size.

"Oh!" she gasped, as everything tightened up, ready for more.

"Yes," he crooned, his lean hips grinding right back, restlessly, near mindlessly, his heavy balls resting against the seam of her buttocks. "So good . . . so fucking good . . ."

Her arms were behind her, palms flat on the coffee table, propping her up. "Fuck me," she begged, rolling her hips into him, feeling every bit like a desirable passionate woman. Something she hadn't felt like in far too long.

"I *am* fucking you, sweetheart." He rose slightly, giving her an eyeful of taut, sweat-sheened abs and revealing the fact that he was still wearing his jeans and boots. That made Stacey even hotter, the look he wore of a man who couldn't bother with getting undressed because he wanted her too badly to spare the time.

It was then that she spotted the strip of condoms on the couch. She glanced down at where they joined with wide eyes. He withdrew then, his cock lined with pulsing veins and shiny from her arousal.

"Condom!" she gasped, as he pushed slowly back inside, raising the temperature of her body enough to make her perspire.

"I'll pull out," he grunted, retreating, then plunging deep again. Harder this time, but not faster. " . . . so damn good . . ."

"Oh god!" Her pussy spasmed in helpless delight. His cock was beautiful to look at, even better to ride. It filled her so full that she could feel all the nuances of it. The furl on the underside of the wide flared head stroked over a highly sensitive spot and her toes pointed. She didn't want to dull any of it, but—"I-I'm not on the pill."

He didn't miss a beat. What would have been a cold shower for most guys did something else to Connor. He tugged her closer to the edge and gave her two rapid strokes. "I can't get you pregnant and I'm clean."

She whimpered as he picked up the pace, his abdominals clenching and releasing in steady measured rhythm. He leaned over her again, pushing her back, rising above her. She stared up at him, melting beneath the heat of his gaze, enamored with the sight of his gorgeous body straining over and inside hers.

"You're the only one," he said roughly. "It's never been real with anyone else."

Stacey's back bowed upward as his driving lunges pushed her closer to orgasm. Releasing his grip on her hair, he set both hands on the table by her shoulders and shafted her cunt in fierce, relentless drives. "You're the only one," he repeated, his gaze unwavering, open.

With her legs around his hips, she came with a cry, writhing beneath him, her toes curling with the intensity of her pleasure. He drew it out expertly, rubbing the head of his cock over and over that sensitive spot inside her, murmuring praise.

Only when she begged weakly, " . . . *no more* . . ." did he yank free and stand over her, gripping his cock and pumping it with his fist until he groaned and cursed and erupted across her heaving breasts in hot, milky spurts.

It was base and raw. Then he gathered her in his arms and sank with her upon the sofa, and it became beautiful and sweet.

Because his body quivered as hers did and his heart beat with the same desperate rhythm as hers.

With his brogue thick with emotion, he whispered her name. Stacey held on tight and fell head over heels.

Chapter 10

"They have the trinity."

Michael frowned and sank onto the stone bench beneath the tree in the Elite Academy courtyard. "That is unfortunate."

Elder Rachel paced as was her wont when agitated. Even in the dream state, the woman was too high strung, yet she remained focused on whatever task was at hand. It was a potent combination—the physical restlessness blended with mental steadfastness.

"It was the damn red hair," she said crossly. "The minions grow unruly and uncooperative within days. Even with the mental chip, they become impossible to control."

"Discard them when they lose their usefulness."

"I know what to do, Elder Sheron. However, one of them dug into their own skull and pulled the chip out. We must assume that the others are capable of such self-infliction."

He knew that, of course. He knew everything stored in her wily brain because he was inside it and because they had colluded for centuries. But he let her talk it out. She hated having him in her mind, so she preferred to act as if he wasn't.

"Leave the completely feral ones to Captains Cross and Bruce," he murmured. "It will keep them busy and you have more important matters to attend to. We need the trinity. You should not have entrusted its retrieval to a minion."

"I had no choice. I had to return to the Twilight for your audience with the Elders. Now that I have 'volunteered' to travel to the mortal plane, we have much greater freedom of movement. I no longer have to pretend to be here when I am actually there."

She spun about, causing her long dark tresses to whip over her shoulder. Michael admired her even as he despised her.

"I cannot trust half the men I took with me," she complained, "because their loyalty is not with you and me, but with the Elder Collective. The minions are wild, but the chip keeps them loyal . . . at least until the Nightmares completely destroy their minds."

Michael brushed a stray leaf off the cuff of his wide sleeve and looked around them, studying Rachel's dream version of the Elite Academy. It had not aged in her mind, retaining the appearance it once possessed when she was a student there. The center courtyard where they met was circular, lined with gravel, and shaded by immense trees. Surrounding the hub were various open-air amphitheatres where combat training took place and in the large building to the south, classrooms were in session.

"It is time to move to the next stage," he said finally.

Rachel stilled, her green eyes widened. "I began to doubt that you would ever proceed."

She had suggested it weeks ago, but he held off. It seemed a waste to use such a tool without devastating effect. Now, the time was right.

"Never doubt me," Sheron said, pushing to his feet. His gaze stayed locked with hers as he pulled up his cowl.

"It will be done as we agreed."

"Excellent." He bowed and moved to the edge of the slipstream. "Until you dream again."

Connor stared down at the dozing woman in his arms and knew he was in deep shit.

His chest was tight and hot, making it difficult to breathe. Every inhale smelled of sweat and sex, every exhale was a moment closer to when he would have to leave.

Stacey was beautiful in near slumber. The tight lines of stress and strain around her mouth and eyes were eased in relaxation, leaving behind a face of youthful loveliness. Creamy smooth skin, dark arched brows, cherry red lips.

He could wake up every day like this. With this woman. In this house. He'd trained enough young men for the Elite that he had confidence in his ability to help Justin, too. Connor knew the type and was familiar with the effects brought on by the lack of a father figure. He had seen it with Aidan. It wouldn't be easy, but for this—he cupped Stacey's cheek with his hand, caressing the curve of her cheekbone with his thumb—for *her*, it would be worth it.

Adjusting her, he pulled her closer and took her mouth, pressing his lips to her softly parted ones. Her moan made his arms tighten around her. He wanted to keep her, discover her, share himself with her. Perhaps what felt good now would feel as good a month from now. A year from now. Years from now.

Promise. There were signs of promise between them, and the thought that it might never come to fruition was difficult for him to bear. It was one thing to be alone when you knew you were happier that way. It was another to be alone when you had someone you wanted to be with.

Licking the seam of Stacey's lips, Connor made love to her lush, soft mouth. Infatuated with the taste of her, he thrust his tongue deep, plunging long and slow, the way he wanted to make love to the rest of her. If only he could get past the feeling of urgency, the sense that at any moment she would be ripped from him and he would lose this chance to enjoy her.

Her hand lifted and slipped into the hair at his nape. The simple touch moved him profoundly for its sheer artlessness. It wasn't a touch designed to arouse. It was a touch intended only to hold him close, to keep him near so she could decimate him with her returning ardor. Stacey gave as good as she got, her tongue stroking along his, her mouth twisting and sucking beneath his, her lips clinging to his.

He pushed to his feet, lifting her with him, never breaking the kiss even as he moved down the hallway to her bedroom.

"Are we going to do it again?" she whispered dreamily into his mouth.

"Hell yeah."

Connor hefted her around to where her legs straddled his hips. It was enough to make him hard as rock, having her curvaceous naked body tucked up tightly against his. She was wet with his cum, a crude claiming that appealed to the primitive beast inside him. No other man could have her. He'd marked her, made her his.

With her arms around his neck, she leaned back and looked down at his cock rising up eagerly between them. "You left the condoms in the living room."

He growled low, wishing he could tell her the truth. From sharing Aidan's dreams, Connor knew that Aidan and Lyssa were certain their species were reproductively incompatible, despite their external similarities. But Connor knew that telling Stacey he was a being from another plane of existence would kill the moment, if not any possibility of a future between them.

"I'll get them," he assured her.

A slow smile curved her mouth and she hugged him, nearly making him stumble as her affection hit him like a physical blow. He carried her into the bathroom and set her down.

"Get in," he said, turning back to return to the living room, "but don't wash. I want to do it."

"Yes, sir," she teased.

She was bending over the tub turning the faucets when he tossed a mock glare over his shoulder. The view was inspiring. He jogged the distance to the condoms, shut the front door and locked it, then jogged the distance back to Stacey.

He heard the shower running as he entered the bedroom and images of water coursing the length of Stacey's luxurious body set his blood on fire. Tapping the automatic release of one boot with the toe of the other, Connor took in the décor. Pale lavender walls, royal purple velvet coverlet, and black sheers covering white plantation shutters made the space rather exotic in comparison to the country look of the living room.

To him it revealed so much about her, the dichotomy between her public spaces and her private one. He wondered if this setting would inspire a different side of Stacey and eager to find out, he shoved his jeans to the floor and strode into the bathroom.

Pausing on the threshold, Connor studiously examined his surroundings. As he had done with every other room in the house, he sought clues to the woman who lived there. The bathroom walls were painted a deep purple—like the comforter in the next room—and the ceiling was decorated with painted silver stars. A hint of whimsy.

"I'm naked and you're looking at the ceiling?" she asked with warm amusement.

He turned his attention to the view of Stacey through the sliding glass shower door. Standing in a cloud of mist, she was his fantasy in the flesh. She slid the door open in invitation.

"I think it might be too small in here for you," she said, blinking water-laden lashes at him as he approached.

"I like tight places," he reminded, climbing into the shower tub with her.

The space was cramped, but he didn't care. It just meant that they were pressed up against each other, which was just the way he wanted it.

Her hands came up and touched his abdomen. His muscles tightened instinctively, responding to her attention.

Her tender fingertips traced over every groove and plane of taut muscle, and he bore her fascination with gritted teeth and aching heart.

"You're so beautiful," she whispered, in what sounded like awe.

He cupped her face, forcing her to look at him. "Tell me how to make this work."

She gazed up at him with liquid, glistening eyes. The green was clear and vivid. Gorgeous. "Connor . . ."

The resignation in her tone drove him crazy. "There has to be a way."

"How?" she asked simply. "How long will you be gone? When will you be back? How long will you stay when you are back?"

"I don't know, damn it." He pushed her head back and devoured her mouth, bruising it, taking it. Thrusting his tongue fast and deep. As steam rose around them in an ever-thickening fog, she whimpered and clung to his waist. "If you want something bad enough—"

"It hurts," she cut off. "That's all. Doesn't mean you get it or can have it."

"Bullshit," he spat, furious with himself, with the Elders, with the lies and deceit that made his leaving unavoidable.

"I told you. I tried to make you listen."

He nuzzled his cheek hard against hers. "Walking away isn't the answer."

She laughed softly. "You're too stubborn."

"Maybe. But I know I can't stand the thought of not having you."

"You're doing wonders for my ego."

"Stop it." He shook her a little. "Don't make light of this."

Stacey sighed and released him. He responded by catching her up and holding all her wet delicious curves against his hardness.

"Connor. Neither of us needs this angst. It's not healthy."

"What angst?" he scoffed. "Teenage girls have angst. I don't."

"You will." She met his gaze head on. "You haven't seen the hell Aidan and Lyssa go through. The struggles to share a phone call between flights. Staying up way past their bedtimes just to hear the other's voice for a moment or two. The pain of separation when he has to travel somewhere and be gone for weeks."

"If they can do it, we can do it."

"No." Shaking her head, she said, "They knew each other before; you and I are strangers. Lyssa is by herself; I come with a child and an ex who may or may not become a more active part of my life. Aidan works for a local collector; you work for . . ." she shrugged, "whoever it is you work for."

Connor's jaw tightened and he rolled his hips into her.

"Very impressive argument," she teased gently. "But the occasional bout of great sex isn't going to keep two people together who are living apart."

Stumped, he tried to come up with counterpoints and failed. He could only stare down at her, scowling. "We can at least try."

"I'm tired of being alone, Connor."

The thought of coming back and seeing her with some-one else made him want to howl. "You wouldn't be alone. I'd be yours, even if I wasn't here."

"A man as highly sexed as you can't be expected to rein it in for me."

"Fuck you," he said tightly, insulted. He set her away from him and reached for the liquid soap. They had to get out of the shower. He could win her over in bed. Torment her there. Drive her mad for him until she would agree to whatever was required for him to slide into her and fill the emptiness. He could ruin her for other men.

"Sorry." She set her hands over his when he cupped her breasts. "I meant that more as a comment on my short-comings, not yours."

"Shortcomings?" He snorted. "I like to fuck. In fact it's one of my favorite activities, followed by honing my glaive, which I usually begin doing while the sheets are still warm."

A finely arched black brow rose.

"Oh yeah, sweetheart," he drawled, squeezing her firm, full tits. "There's even a joke about my first loves being my swords—the one in my hand and the one between my legs. There's no post-coital cuddling. Women want me for sex, nothing more. And that's always worked just fine for me."

He watched the emotions that swept across her expres-sive features. "Ah," he murmured, smiling, "you're think-ing about last night, right? I held you on the couch. I slept with you in my arms. I cuddled with you a few minutes ago and I can't stop touching you now."

Catching her hand, Connor pulled it down and thrust his erection into it. "That's sexual interest." He pulled her hand back up and set it over his heart. "This tightening in my chest that you can't see? That's something I've never felt before. You've got something no one else has. You don't have a shortcoming, sweetheart. You have an advantage."

Stacey's lips quivered alarmingly and his stomach knotted further.

"With you, I didn't even think about whetting my sword," he rushed forward.

She covered her mouth.

"Well, not the metal sword," he corrected gruffly, knowing he was screwing this all up but unsure of how to fix it. "I mean *you're* wet and my other sword . . . I mean I thought about wetting *that* sword—"

Her lovely face scrunched up and he begged, "Don't cry!"

He wrapped his arms around her and patted her shaking back awkwardly. "Oh man. I suck at this. I'm not trying to make you feel bad. I meant that as a compliment. It's my problem I'm nuts for you, not yours. I—"

Her lips pressed ardently to his nipple, then she ran her tongue over it in a slow, heated swipe. He stiffened, staring down at her with wide eyes.

She was laughing at him.

"That was beautiful," she mock sniffled, her hands cupping his ass.

His brows rose. "Yeah?"

"Oh yeah. I'm pretty sure I have never made a man's chest tight before." Her smile was pure sunshine. "I like it."

"How about the other part?"

Stacey laughed. "You know damn well I like the other part." Her voice lowered provocatively. "If we hurry up and get out of the shower, I will show you how much."

Connor considered that a moment, somewhat lost in the barrage of emotions he felt. Something like joy. Maybe hope. He hid how twisted up he was by teasing. "You're not just using me for my body, right?"

"Sure I am." She cupped his balls in both hands. "But when you're gone and I'm waiting desperately by the phone, I'll be thinking about more than your swords."

Stacey followed Connor out of the bathroom at her insistence. She wanted to ogle his bare behind. Lucky for her, it was a view well worth ogling. The man had legs honed by strenuous activity. Gorgeous legs. Long and leanly muscled. His ass was a perfect complement. Taut and firm. Tight. Flexing with every step. With dimples on either side.

Yum.

And there, between his legs, the occasional glimpse of his heavy balls. Denuded. Delicious. Perhaps if he weren't erect, she could see the head of his cock, too, but he was rocked and cocked. Ready. For her.

How did she get so lucky? She couldn't shake the feeling that it was all too good to be true. There had to be something wrong with him. Stacey Daniels did not wind up with perfect men. There was always something screwy with them. Something majorly whacked that prevented any possibility of a relationship. Like Tommy, who wanted to be eighteen years old forever. Or Tom Stein, who wanted to live a "green" life in the desert, surviving off solar energy and rain water. Stacey was pretty sure that the gene that created hotness on the outside also created misfiring brain cells on the inside.

She sighed. Connor was ultra-hot. The finest looking man she'd ever met. As perfect as the rear view was, it barely kept up with the front view. Where were his flaws? His inability to talk about his feelings? Hell, she didn't like flowery speech. Honesty was more of a turn-on for her than pretty phrases.

Connor reached her bed, turned to face her, and caught her up in his big brawny arms.

She loved the feeling of being small. Of being protected and cherished.

"That was hot," he rumbled.

"Hmm?" Her eyes closed as she relished the feel of his hard body against hers. The light dusting of hair on his chest tickled her nipples and the smell of his skin, undiluted by her bath soap, did crazy things to her heart rate.

"Feeling you watching me."

"You're gorgeous," she breathed, raising her lids just enough to see him.

"Before today, I considered my looks a convenience to getting laid."

Stacey laughed softly, appreciating how bluntly open he was. "I'm sure it has been."

His firm lips nuzzled against her temple. "Now, I'm grateful my looks are the kind you like."

"Oh yes." She nipped at his chin with her teeth. "I like."

Connor spun abruptly and tossed her onto the coverlet. She bounced with a squeal and then he was on her, crawling over her in a cage of hard, luscious masculinity. He started with a lick between her toes, then pressed a kiss to her ankle, then lifted her leg and nibbled in the hollow behind her knee. It tickled and she laughed.

"That giggle of yours makes me hot," he rumbled, pausing to stare at her.

Rolling her eyes, Stacey pointed out, "Everything makes you hot. You're a sex machine."

"Oh yeah?" He gripped her inner thighs and spread her legs open, exposing her to his gaze. "I distinctly remember attempting to call a cab when you attacked me and demanded sex."

"After you badgered me into it!" She bit back a laugh when he arched a brow at her. She was amazed she was even capable of conversation with him poised above her pussy with a wolfish gleam in his eyes. Thing was, she'd never been silly in bed before. She liked it.

"How does your saying to me, 'You're not getting out of this now' constitute badgering?"

"The badgering came before that."

Connor snorted. "I've never badgered a woman for sex in my life."

"You also didn't fight when I gave in," she argued, sticking her tongue out playfully.

His aqua gaze darkened and heated at the sight. "Gave in?" he scoffed. "I'm a guy, sweetheart. Throw gorgeous pussy at us and we're not going to say no."

Her mouth fell open on a choked laugh. "I did *not* throw my pussy at you."

"Umm . . . yeah." He winked. Added in combination with his boyishly charming smile, it was devastating to a woman's equilibrium. "You did. Nymphomaniac. Jees, can't get a break around this place. Sex last night. Sex again today. Sex right now . . ." He sighed dramatically.

"Oh, far be it from me to fuck you to death," she said, crossing her arms over her chest. "Let's just go eat pie."

Connor stuck his lower lip out in a mock pout. "I was going to eat something else."

Considering where he was, she got the idea. "Nah. That's okay. This nymphomaniac is amazingly not in the mood for sex anymore."

A total bald-faced lie. She was slick and swollen. When he glanced down skeptically and then grinned, she knew he could see it.

"I can put you in the mood," he purred.

"Puh-leaze." She faked a yawn.

His low growl made her laugh.

"You're going to pay for that," he threatened, tickling her.

"Ah! Stop it!" She tried to roll away from him and succeeded only in ending up on her stomach, a distinct advantage for him.

He came over her immediately, laughing. *Laughing.* His lips to her ear, he said, "I'm going to make you beg me for it."

Stacey shivered with anticipation. "I'd like to see you try." Boy, would she ever!

"No trying involved, sweetheart." He licked the shell of her ear, then dipped inside. She grew hotter, wetter. As if he knew, he pushed his big hand between her legs and stroked her. "Yum," he said. "Someone's horny already."

"Not me." She gasped as he found her clit and rubbed in gentle circles.

He hummed a skeptical noise and she buried her smile in her pillow. She felt him move, felt the bed dip and sway, and then his tongue, hot and rough coursing the length of her spine. She gasped and writhed, the sensation both ticklish and arousing. Connor pinned her hips still and licked in the dimple at the small of her back. "Stop wiggling," he ordered.

"I was hoping you'd move so I could get up and get some pie."

Connor grumbled something and bit her butt cheek. Then he rolled her over, angled his cock down, and pushed inside her.

Stacey whimpered and arched upward. God, it felt so damn good. He was huge everywhere, even there, and the sensation of being stretched to her limits was incredible. He planted his hands on either side of her head and glared down at her. It was an intimidating picture he made, but the warm amusement in his eyes belied the tough image.

"So deliciously tiiiggghhhttt . . ." he said, rolling his hips into her. "I can do this all day."

She gasped when he flexed inside her. "You might be able to talk me into that."

He pulled out slowly, then returned in a long torturous glide. "I thought you wanted pie."

"Umm . . . I changed my mind."

Connor pumped out and then in again. As he fucked her slow and with such skill, her eyes slid closed on a low moan. He reared up and kneeled, draping her legs over his muscular thighs, rocking back and forth. The thick head of his cock rubbed inside her, stroking across a bundle of nerves that made her nipples tighten and stab into the air. He struck hard and she cried out as he found the end of her, the mixture of pleasure and pain curling her toes.

"You're so deep," she slurred, cupping her breasts to ease their swollen ache.

"I want to get deeper." His abdomen laced tight as he grabbed her hips and plunged to the root, grinding against her. He was thicker at the base, which caused her clit to tilt downward and catch added friction.

"Connor!" Her head thrashed in near delirium, unable to bear the depth and leisurely pace of his fucking. It was unbelievably good. Impossibly good. A few more strokes like that and she was going to have the orgasm of her life. "Yes . . . um, yes . . ."

He pulled free and slipped off the bed.

Stacey struggled up onto her elbows and gaped at him. "Where are you going?"

He looked over his shoulder and blinked innocently. "I'm going to get you some pie. You said you wanted some."

"Y-you . . . w-what . . . *now* . . . ?"

"I wouldn't want to force you into sex or anything."

"Get back here!"

He grinned and paused at the door, lounging insolently into the jamb. Buck-assed naked with a full raging hard-on, he made a stunning picture. "Nympho," he teased.

"Come on!" she cajoled impatiently. "Please."

"Was that begging?"

Her gaze narrowed. "Get. Over. Here. Now."

He crossed his arms and studied her intently. "What will you do when I'm gone and you're horny?"

"Play with myself," she said easily. "But that's not nearly as much fun as playing with you and you're here."

"Do it," he urged, his hot gaze dropping to her lewdly spread legs. "I want to watch."

She considered that a long moment, watching him watching her. The way his lips parted and his breathing sped up told her the idea of witnessing her masturbating turned him on.

"Will you jack off to this memory when you're away?" she asked, pushing her splayed fingers through the damp curls of her sex.

Connor licked his lips and took himself in hand. "I'm ready to jack off to it now."

The pads of her fingers rested over her engorged clit and she rubbed in languid circles, shivering from both the lack of his body heat and her building arousal. She'd need a faster pace to reach orgasm, but that wasn't the point of the exercise. The point was to get Connor in a rut, so he'd come back and finish what he started. She moaned and his entire body jerked.

"Fuck," he rasped, straightening.

"Oh!" Her neck arched back, thrusting her breasts into the air. She rubbed harder and a little faster, reaching lower to gather the slickness at the slit of her pussy, then rising up to lubricate her motions.

Then his fingers were there, pushing inside her, thrusting. Fucking. She was panting, twisting and he was standing there next to her. His gorgeous face flushed, his jaw taut, his irises swallowed by dilated pupils. His attention was between her legs, where he was fingering her expertly, where she was fondling herself franticly. His cock was hard as stone, the tip an angry red and glistening with the semen that leaked from the tiny hole.

"Let me suck you," she begged, her mouth watering at the thought.

With a rough, edgy sound Connor returned to the bed, lying lengthwise, his cock by her mouth, her pussy at his chest. They rolled until they faced one another, their heights so disparate, but perfect for this.

Stacey gripped his magnificent cock with two hands and angled it down to her waiting mouth. Her tongue touched the hot tip and he cursed viciously but didn't lose the rhythm of his fingers. He added his callused thumb to the mix, manipulating her clit with just the right pressure to set her off.

She climaxed with a muffled cry, her mouth full, her tongue fluttering rapidly over the sensitive spot just beneath the crown of his cock. He roared her name, coming hard, hips bucking in his orgasmic frenzy. Stacey took it all, every drop, sucking deeply with hollowing cheeks, drinking him down with open-throated delight.

"No more, sweetheart," he murmured huskily. "You're killing me."

Stacey released him only when he pushed her head weakly away. He curled around and joined her, wrapping her in his arms and tossing a leg over both of hers.

Feeling cherished, she set her cheek next to his madly racing heart and fell asleep.

Chapter 11

It took a moment for Connor to realize what woke him. He was fully alert and sliding away from Stacey's warm body when it registered—footsteps approaching the front door. The window behind the scrolled wrought iron headboard overlooked the far end of the porch, and he pushed aside the sheer black curtain and peeked between the shutters.

Aidan and Lyssa were ascending the short stairs.

Cursing under his breath, he turned around and reached for his pants.

"Who is it?" Stacey asked in a sleep-husky rasp.

"Mom and Dad," he muttered.

"Huh? Oh . . . Ugh." She sat up, looking tousled and well fucked—kiss-swollen lips, pink cheeks, rosy skin. "Do you think telling them to mind their own business will work?"

"It damn well better." He zipped up and held out a hand to her. Tugging her from the bed, he ran a quick admiring glance down the length of her body, cupped a swaying breast, and kissed her passionately. "You get dressed. I'll get the door."

He turned away and she swatted him on the ass. "Yes, sir."

Tossing a mock glare over his shoulder, Connor left the bedroom, traversed the hall, and unlocked the front door.

Aidan took one look at his bare chest and feet, and scowled. "Asshole."

"Shithead," Connor retorted.

"I take no responsibility for him," Aidan said to Lyssa. "He fucks up, it's not my fault."

She patted his arm. "Calm down, honey."

Connor smiled at Lyssa. "Hi."

Her returning smile was just as sweet as she was. "Hi. I smell apple pie."

Laughing, Connor stepped back, pulling the door open wide. It was late afternoon, the hour when the sky was more orange than blue and the hottest part of the day was behind them. "I'm sure Stacey will be slicing it up soon. She's been talking about that pie all day."

"Have you moved in now?" Aidan snapped.

"Dude." Connor shook his head. "You need to get laid or take vitamins or something."

"He doesn't need to get laid," Lyssa assured, grinning.

"Yes, I do," Aidan argued, "and if you blow it for me, Bruce, I'm kicking your ass."

"Wow." Both of Connor's brows rose. "You must really have it going on, Lyssa. He's awfully anxious about pissing you off."

She offered a saucy shrug. "What can I say?"

"Hey, Doc." Stacey entered the living room from the hallway. "Want some apple pie?"

"Told ya," Connor said.

"Can we talk, Bruce?" Aidan said tightly, gesturing toward the front door.

"I don't know. Can we?" Connor set his hands on his hips. "You don't look capable of talking. You look like you want to bitch."

Aidan stood there for a moment, still and tense. Then a faint hint of a smile touched the corner of his mouth. "Please."

"Aw, alright."

"Want me to cut you a slice?" Stacey called after him.

"Hell, yeah." He winked at her. "I want to try some of that pie-that's-better-than-sex."

"I didn't say that!" she protested, blushing.

"You must really *not* have it going on," Aidan ribbed. "Stace's pie is good, but it's not *that* good."

"Watch it."

Aidan's laughter followed Connor out the screen door and onto the porch. Moving to stand at the railing, Connor said, "Before you get started, my sex life is none of your damn business."

"We'll debate that later. Right now I gotta tell you about what happened when I woke up."

There was excitement in Aidan's voice, which caught and held Connor's attention. "Yeah?"

"I found a letter I wrote to myself."

Connor blinked. "O-kay . . ."

"While I was sleeping."

"Wager." Admiration filled Connor at the thought. The lieutenant was wily and resourceful, two traits that any officer would appreciate finding in the soldiers under his command.

"Yes. I always liked him. Smart kid."

Wager was a few centuries beyond being a "kid," but Connor got the idea.

Aidan ran a hand through his hair. In the Twilight, he'd always kept it short. The inky locks were longer now than Connor could ever remember seeing them. The look softened the captain's features and blended with the glow of happiness visible whenever he looked at Lyssa. He was a changed man, a previously hopeless man who now had hope.

"What did it say?" Connor asked.

"He found traces of a bug inside the files you downloaded from the temple." Aidan walked over to the swinging bench and sat.

Turning, Connor rested his hip against the railing. "A *bug?*"

"Yes, a virus or Trojan program that's been monitoring everything the Elders have been doing."

"Eavesdropping?"

Aidan looked at him grimly. "Yeah."

"So everything we know, someone else also knows?"

"Looks that way."

Gripping the wooden slats behind him, Connor looked across the side-lawn to the neighbor's yard. He exhaled harshly. "Any idea how long the bug has been there?"

"The letter didn't say. Wager is tracing it, but cautions

us against holding our breaths. He says it'll take some time and there is no guarantee of success."

"Well, someone else out there doesn't trust the Elders either. Maybe that's a good thing for us."

"Or maybe not."

"True."

"The letter also mentioned that your dreams with Sheron could be true. Wager found a file on a program called 'dream incursion.' Something about enhancing dreams with information that would become memorable. He's working on that lead, too."

"Poor guy," Connor muttered. "How in hell did he end up with the Elite? His brain has got to be bored with all the chest thumping."

Aidan laughed. "He's too hotheaded for a desk assignment. I asked him once why he joined the Elite. He said it was his first love and the rest was just a hobby."

"Some hobby."

The low rumble of a car's engine drew both of their gazes to the road. Just beyond the chain link fence that marked Stacey's property, a black sedan with dark tinted windows cruised slowly along then turned into the driveway.

The screen door opened and the girls exited the house backwards, balancing small desert plates atop each hand. Both men spared only fleeting glances in their direction.

"Who is that?" Stacey asked, noting how both Connor and Aidan seemed unduly interested in the approaching vehicle.

Aidan stood and glanced at her, frowning. "You don't recognize the car?"

She shook her head.

"Get in the house," Connor ordered, moving to stand between her and the visitor.

For a moment, Stacey contemplated the effectiveness of pointing out that she wasn't one to be ordered around. In the end, she stepped around Connor and set the two slices of pie she was carrying on top of the two-by-four railing.

"It's my house," she pointed out. "Whoever it is wants to see me. Or they're lost. Most likely lost, because—"

"I've got this, Cross," Connor interjected darkly. "You take care of Lyssa."

Stacey fell silent as Aidan leaped to his feet and pushed Lyssa roughly into the house.

Connor caught her arm and tugged her back behind him as the car rolled to a stop and the rear driver's side door opened. Stacey swatted at him, loving that he was overprotective but also finding it annoying. Too much of anything was too much and . . .

Her mouth fell open as a woman beautiful enough to put Angelina Jolie out of a job unfolded from the backseat. The gal had black hair and green eyes like Stacey, but unlike Stacey, she was tall and willowy with the defined muscles of a body builder. She was also drop-dead gorgeous—blessed with perfectly symmetrical facial features and softly tanned skin. Dressed in a gray sleeveless tunic and loose-legged pants, her garments reminded Stacey of the ones Connor had been wearing when he arrived on Lyssa's doorstep.

"I have no idea who that is," Stacey said.

"Captain Bruce," the woman called out in greeting, smiling in a way that made Stacey's skin crawl. She had the same accent that Connor and Aidan had, which only increased Stacey's unease.

"You know her?" Stacey asked, heart sinking. No way could she compete with a woman who looked like that.

"Rachel," Connor rejoined.

The grim tone of Connor's voice didn't help settle Stacey, like she would have thought. Yeah, she was glad he wasn't happy to see Rachel, but on the other hand, drama scenes were not her cuppa tea.

"Look how sweetly you protect your human lover," Rachel drawled, resting her arm elegantly along the top of the open car door. "I always said the need for sex was a weakness unique to male members of the Elite."

"What the fuck is she talking about?" Stacey muttered. "Who is that?" Her eyes widened. "Oh my god! You're not married are you?"

"What?" Connor barked, glaring at her. "To *her*? Are you nuts?"

"To anyone?"

"No!"

Rachel cleared her throat. "Excuse me. Can you argue after I conclude my business? I have a long drive ahead of me and I would like to 'hit the road' as they say."

Aidan came back. He handed something to Connor, then looked at Stacey. "You need to come inside, Stace."

Stacey glanced down at the object in Connor's hand and comprehension dawned.

"Oh, I get it!" She grinned sheepishly. "This is about the sword!"

"Sweetheart," Connor bit out between clenched teeth. "Go inside the damn house. Now."

"Bossy, aren't they?" Rachel said, laughing. "You can come with me, sweetheart. I have some . . . *friends* . . . who would love to meet you."

"You'll have to kill me, Rachel," Connor challenged, "to get to her."

Rachel tossed her hair over her shoulder and laughed. "I know! Isn't that delicious? As impatient as I was for the Key to be found, getting you and Cross in the bargain makes it all worth it."

Totally confused, Stacey's gaze drifted to the man in the driver's seat. He looked like a dude from *Men in Black*. Black suit, blacker sunglasses. Something about him was even weirder than Rachel's Cruella de Ville-vibe, even though he didn't move and bore no expression on his face.

"But claiming the Key now would be a bit like putting the cart before the horse," Rachel said with a careless wave of her hand. "So you can enjoy your unfortunate humans a little bit longer."

"Why does she keep saying 'human' like that?" Stacey whispered fiercely, disliking the other woman immensely. Rachel was so damned smug and nasty. And the way she set Connor and Aidan on edge didn't recommend her too highly either.

"What do you want?" Connor asked, moving to stand by the steps as if he dared anyone to pass him and gain entry to the house. Considering he had a huge unsheathed sword in his hand, the intimidation was highly successful. At least for Stacey.

"You have something that belongs to me, Bruce. I want it back."

He descended the first step. "Fuck you."

Rachel's grin widened. "I would not come empty-handed, surely you know that?"

"You show us yours first," Connor rumbled before turning his head and hissing to Aidan, "Get her in the house!"

Aidan caught her upper arm in a relentless grip and tugged her toward the door.

"Fine." Stacey went. "But I'm watching through the window."

"I want the trinity," Rachel said.

Connor shrugged. "No idea what that is. Looks like you're shit out of luck."

Stacey paused at the door. "Stop provoking her! She's a nut."

"Perhaps this will jog your memory," Rachel said. She looked into the backseat. "Get out."

The other rear door opened and a man stepped out.

"Oh my god," Stacey breathed, her hand falling away from the door handle as she recognized the man wearing a black turtleneck sweater and ski pants. "That's Tommy! What the fuck is he doing with them?"

The tension that gripped Connor's large frame was palpable. "Cross . . . that's Stacey's ex."

Tommy stood next to the car in an obvious daze, his eyes sightless and uncomprehending.

The next moment the driver moved, reaching over to the front passenger seat and yanking a bound and gagged body into view.

Stacey screamed, doubling over at the sight of Justin's terrified eyes and tear-stained face.

Rachel's smile was chilling. "So, now I have shown you

mine. And he will stay mine until you return the trinity to me."

Goaded by instinct, Stacey ran for the stairs and her son. Connor's arm thrust out lightning quick, slamming her back. She yelled her fury and frustration, flailing as she went down, losing her breath as Aidan caught her and held her writhing body with steely arms. She arched and twisted, kicking her legs madly, but he was too big and too strong.

Rachel reached into her pocket and withdrew a cell phone. She tossed it at Connor, who caught it and held it to his chest. "I will call you with instructions."

"If something happens to the boy," Connor warned, his voice low and deadly earnest. "I'll torture you before I kill you."

"Ooh!" She gave a vixen-ish little shake of her shoulders. "Sounds delicious." Her lovely face hardened. "I want that trinity, Captain. See that I get it or the kid will pay."

"Nooooo!" The sound that left Stacey's body was inhuman. It was an animal's cry, one filled with pain and frustration and a mother's fear for her child. She struggled within Aidan's unyielding grasp, jerking and scratching to be freed. *"Justin!"*

She watched in wide-eyed horror as her son's panicked writhing mirrored her own. Justin's bound hands lifted and struck out, knocking the sunglasses from his captor's face, revealing a visage that stopped her heart. The man hit back, knocking Justin unconscious. Then he turned his black gaze to Stacey, grinning with a yawing cavern of jagged teeth, taking pleasure in her torment and revulsion.

Her cries echoed around them, then Aidan's hand was over her mouth, muffling her, his deep voice murmuring to her.

Why weren't they doing anything? Why were they letting that bitch climb back into the car and shut the door? Why was Tommy just standing there, barely blinking as the car reversed out of the driveway with their child inside it? Why was Aidan restraining her, gagging her, crooning to her as if all the promises of safety and retribution he was making would calm her?

The thing in the driver's seat was driving away with her baby and she could only watch, imprisoned by the arms of someone she'd thought was a friend.

Aidan held her until the car was out of sight, then he let her go. Her shaky legs caused her to stumble and fall to her knees, then she scrambled to her feet, pushing past Connor when he attempted to restrain her. She ran to Tommy and beat at him, yelled at him, shook him.

"You goddamned junkie!" she screamed, slapping his face with every bit of strength she possessed. "You worthless piece of shit!"

Then she was running, running for the life of her son, clearing her property and chasing the black sedan down the road. It was quickly beyond sight, but she didn't stop. She couldn't stop. She ran until she couldn't run anymore, sinking to the ground and crying. Wailing. Hiccupping.

"Stacey." Connor knelt beside her, his eyes red and watery and filled with such compassion.

"No!" she shouted. "You do *not* g-get to cry. You let them t-take him . . ." She slapped at his bare chest, then pounded her fists against it. "How c-could you l-let them take him? How could y-you?"

"I'm sorry," he whispered, making no effort to defend himself from her attack. "I'm so sorry, Stace. There was nothing I could have done. If there had been any way to take him back alive, I would have. You have to believe me."

"You didn't even try!" she sobbed. "You didn't even try."

Stacey crumpled into his lap, her blurry gaze fixed on the unpaved road. His feet were bare and bleeding from coming after her. Her heart clenched at the sight, which only pissed her off further.

Connor picked her up and carried her back. She had no strength left to resist, but she found no comfort in his embrace.

Her precious child was gone.

Chapter 12

Lyssa was crying on the couch when Connor returned to the house with Stacey. Aidan was pacing. Tommy was restrained with duct tape in a chair by the door. With his mind connected to the Twilight, Stacey's ex couldn't be trusted. The Elders had once attempted to kill Lyssa through a sleepwalker, which had alerted them to the fact that such machinations were possible.

For his part, Connor felt helpless, a state of being that was anathema to his mental health. Stacey's pain was gnawing at him, driving him half-mad with bloodlust and restless fury.

"Oh god, Stace!" Lyssa pushed to her feet as the screen door shut silently behind them. She hurried over, embracing her best friend as soon as Connor set her down. "I'm so s-sorry! This is all my fault."

Stacey shook her head. "You couldn't do anything." Her venomous gaze moved from Aidan to Tommy to Connor, who flinched. "Too bad we didn't have some big strong men around," she sneered, brushing past everyone on the way to the phone.

"Stacey." Lyssa's voice was low and pleading. "You can't call for help."

"Why the fuck not?" she demanded, reaching for the handset with a violently shaking hand. "Because the cops might come out here and think, 'Hmm? Look at these two brawny, ex-Special Forces guys who didn't do a *goddamned thing* to stop a kidnapping!'"

Lifting his chin, Connor knew she had every right to be pissed based on the information she had, but her derision still wounded deeply. Not his pride or his ego, both of which had suffered more than a few dents over the course of his lifetime, but his heart, which had never been engaged enough to feel pain.

The damn thing was killing him now.

"You don't know her like we do, Stacey," he said gently. "There was nothing we could have done that would still assure Justin's safety."

"Bullshit!" Stacey's eyes were wide and dark, the dilated pupils leaving only a faint ring of the brilliant green irises. Her skin and lips were pale, her hands shaking. "Either one of you—*alone!*—could have taken out *both* her and that freak with the mask on!"

"Are you sure there were only two of them?" he asked, making her pause. "With those tinted windows it was impossible to see into the backseat."

"There was someone else in the back," Aidan assured. "Someone closed the door on the passenger side after Tommy got out."

A frown marred Stacey's brow as she considered this.

Connor pressed on, needing her to understand, "Justin is valuable to her because of *you*, Stace. Rachel was prepared to spar, with the goal being to kill Justin and take you instead. That would up the ante, and trust us, Rachel likes sky-high antes. She was standing next to the open car door for a reason. I'm positive she had her glaive right there within reach, waiting for one of us to make a move."

"What the hell kind of antiquities are you dealing in," she snapped, "that would be valuable enough to kidnap someone over them?"

"Hey." Lyssa spoke softly, stepping closer and putting her arm around Stacey's quivering shoulders. "Let's go in the kitchen, and I'll tell you everything."

"I need to call the damn cops."

"Let me explain first. Then, if you still feel like you need the police, I'll drive you over there myself."

"What is *wrong* with you people?" Stacey yelled, her voice hoarse. "My son is gone and you want me to do nothing?"

"No," Connor murmured, his gut knotted painfully. "We want you to believe in us—your friends. The people who l-lo—"

The word strangled in his throat, his insides too raw to bare himself to further scorn. He'd failed her. Even though he couldn't have done any more than he did without jeopardizing Justin's life, he'd still failed to shield her from pain.

Love.

Was that the right word? He cared for her. Wanted to be with her. Hated to see her so devastated. He wanted her smiles and her laughter, wanted her gentle touches and breathless cries of pleasure. He wanted to get to know her and share himself in return. Was that love?

Perhaps it was the seeds of it. The first sprouting. Would it wither now and die? Or could he repair the damage and have a chance to watch it grow?

"I'm your best friend, Stace." Lyssa's sweet voice held a note of steel that cut into Connor's thoughts. "I love you. I love Justin. I want him back as much as you do."

Connor's chest grew tight as Stacey broke down and cried, leaning heavily into her friend, her black curls blending with Lyssa's blonde strands. It was the sound of hopelessness and despair, and it ripped him to shreds. She was his woman. The only one he'd ever had. It was his job to protect her and keep her safe. Instead he introduced her to the danger that wounded her so gravely.

"Bruce!"

He tore his gaze away from Stacey's back as she left the living room and looked at Aidan. "What?"

"Pull it together and let's fix this."

"I am together." He wasn't. He felt like he was falling apart. Such an odd feeling to be scattered. His heart in one place, his brain in another, his body tense with the need to give chase. "We can track them through the cell phone. McDougal has the capability."

Aidan nodded, his features tight with strain. "Comes in handy when you get an out-of-the-blue offer for a priceless artifact. We track down the dealer and verify that they're legit before proceeding with the transaction. But that's not going to help us figure out what Rachel wants."

Because of the time Connor had spent inside Aidan's slipstream, he had a mental storage of Aidan's memories.

He'd been rifling through them ever since Rachel had made the demand and he couldn't find anything resembling a trinity in the recollections. To Aidan's knowledge, none of the artifacts he'd recovered were the item Rachel wanted.

Connor ran both hands through his hair, tortured by the sounds of muffled crying coming from the kitchen. "Rachel is either completely insane or she's talking about that dirt clod you've got."

"Shit."

"Told you I had it together," he muttered.

Stacey screeched and something made of glass broke in the other room. He winced. If Lyssa was telling her about the Twilight, things were about to get a whole lot worse.

"I've got the duffle in the car," Aidan muttered, before sprinting out the door.

Staring down at the cell phone in his hand, Connor started a checklist of necessary items in his mind. He'd need transportation, clothes, a cooler with food and drink . . .

"What the hell have you two done to my best friend?" Stacey asked coldly, entering the room.

Connor squared his shoulders and faced her head on. "We saved her life."

"Bullshit." Her eyes snapped with emerald fire, which was actually a relief after the blankness he'd seen before. "You've got her convinced that you're dream fighters and she's some prophet of doom and gloom."

"Prophecy," he corrected. "And we're Elite Warriors, Stacey. We don't fight dreams, we protect them."

The quivering of her lower lip was the only sign of her distress. Her shoulders were back, her chin tilted stubbornly. Ready to take on the world alone.

"I knew there was something wrong with you," she said bitterly. "Too good to be true. What do you want?"

He arched a brow.

"Come on," she coaxed with a sneer. "Two gorgeous guys appear on our doorsteps out of nowhere. They have no past and my kid gets snatched. Coincidence? I don't think so."

It took a moment for her accusation to sink in. Then, "You think I did this?" He stared at her a moment, slack jawed. "You think *I* had a hand in kidnapping Justin?"

"It's the only thing that makes any sense to me."

"Who said this shit has to make sense?"

Connor lunged and caught her to him, thrusting his free hand in her hair and tugging her neck back, forcing her to look at him. "We *made love*. I was *inside* you. How can you accuse me of something so heinous after what we've shared?"

"It was sex," she dismissed. But her chest was heaving against his and tears filled her eyes.

Prepared to do anything—*anything*—to win her trust back, he released her, then caught her hand in his and dragged her to the kitchen.

Lyssa waited on the threshold, but quickly stepped out of the way. Connor walked up to the wooden knife block on the white ceramic tiled counter and withdrew a blade. With gritted teeth, he turned to face Stacey and slashed diagonally across his chest, cutting himself from shoulder to abdomen.

She screamed as blood welled and ran down his torso. He tossed the knife in the stainless steel sink and said grimly, "Don't take your eyes off me."

The burning began and then the itching. His skin healed itself almost instantaneously. It had been a shallow wound, quickly mended, unlike Aidan's deep gash, which had taken hours to resolve.

"Holy shit," she breathed, stumbling as her knees gave out.

Catching her, he helped her to the nearby table in the breakfast nook. She touched his skin, swiping through the blood to see that there was no mark left behind. Aidan returned at that moment and set the black duffle down next to her elbow.

He unzipped the bag and pulled out the book he'd stolen from the Elders and the cloth-wrapped bundle. "We need to clean this thing off, Bruce, and see if we can find mention of whatever-it-is in here."

"I have to head to McDougal's," Connor said, "before Rachel calls."

"You can't go. You'll never get past security."

"Watch me." Connor smiled grimly. "I can't read the language of the Ancients—I slept through those classes— but I can break into anywhere and kick the shit out of anyone."

Aidan appeared prepared to argue.

"Trust me, Aidan. It's better this way. Instead of you risking your job, you can play the victim of a kidnapping or something like that. You'll be blameless."

"It's a fucked-up plan," Aidan muttered.

"Hey, I learned those from the best."

Growling low, Aidan nevertheless said, "Go. I'll work on figuring out why she wants this damn trinity so bad."

Stacey reached for the book and opened it, running her fingers over the text. "What is this?"

Needing to have some connection to her, Connor set his hand on her shoulder and leaned over. "Prior to the creation of virtual databases, our people documented our history in texts, just as you do."

"You can't read this?" she asked, her gaze locked on the turning pages.

"No. Our present-day language is based on it, just as your language is rooted in Latin, but only scholars and the overly curious—like Cross—know enough of its pure form to make sense of it."

"Jesus," she whispered. "I feel like I'm losing my mind."

He glanced up at Aidan who caught his eye and said, "We'll take care of her."

Connor hated that he couldn't be the one to comfort her, but he knew his place in Stacey's life was tenuous at best. She needed consolation and security, and he knew she wouldn't turn to him for either. The best he could do was manage the logistics and dirty work of Justin's retrieval.

He nodded. "Thanks. I'm off to get the things we need."

Stacey twisted in the chair to look up at him. "What things? What do we need?"

"I'm going after your son. I'll need certain equipment to do it."

Hope filled her eyes. "I'm going with you."

"No way," he said firmly. "It's not safe. You need—"

"Don't tell me it's not safe!" She lunged to her feet. "If

Justin is there, I'm there. Did you see the terror on his face? Did you see that freak sitting next to him, hiding behind that fucking mask so I can't identify him to the police?"

"A mask?" Lyssa frowned.

"Yeah, Doc. A mask. With black eyes and fake vampire teeth. It scared me just looking at it. I can't imagine what my baby is going through—" Stacey's voice choked into silence.

Connor caught her close, unable to do otherwise, but she struggled and broke free. She rounded the island, as if that barrier could keep him from her.

His jaw tensed as her rejection cut deeply.

"A mask . . ." Lyssa whispered through white lips. "Oh no!"

Connor could see that she understood the implication. He had no idea how Rachel was controlling the Nightmare-infected Guardian, but regardless, he doubted the leash was tight enough to ensure Justin's safety for long.

The clock was ticking.

Shoving the cell phone in his pocket, Connor turned to leave. "I'm out."

Aidan sank into the chair in front of the duffel.

"I'll make coffee," Lyssa said.

"I'm going to pack," Stacey muttered, leaving the kitchen.

Connor gritted his teeth and ran out the door, preparing himself for the argument ahead. He was not going to risk Stacey. Best she get used to that idea now.

He climbed into Lyssa's Roadster and took off.

Chapter 13

The drive from the massive wrought iron security gate to the front of the McDougal mansion was not a short one. It was at least two miles long and it wended up the rather steep hill in a series of sharp turns. Cameras on poles turned their eyes to mark Connor's progress, a precaution the McDougal security team made no effort to hide.

Having seen Aidan's memories, Connor knew the first time his friend had come here he'd been slightly intimidated by the rather forbidding welcome. Months later, it still put Aidan on edge, but the job was uniquely suited to their needs so he managed. A bit of discomfort was worth the money the job paid and the unlimited travel expenses.

Connor didn't have the luxury or inclination to be nervous about the task ahead. Stacey and Justin needed him and his personal discomfort didn't matter as far as he was concerned.

He rounded the circular drive and parked Lyssa's BMW in the parking spot designated with Aidan's name. The main house was located around the next bend. This smaller building was set aside for Aidan's use.

When Aidan was ready to work, a team of six assistants would be on hand to help him. Since he was supposed to be in Mexico, the building was deserted, which suited Connor's aims perfectly. He was going to "borrow" the items he needed. He was pretty certain McDougal would consider it stealing.

Pulling Aidan's keys out of his pocket, Connor unlocked the heavy metal door. He pushed it open and the lights came on, illuminating a linoleum-lined hallway flanked by rooms suiting various purposes on either side.

In some respects, it reminded him of both the rock cavern in the Twilight and the private gallery in the Temple of the Elders where the floor dissolved into multi-colored swirls and glimpses of a starry expanse of space. Fanciful, he knew, to compare this sterile human environment to the mysteries of the Twilight, but he couldn't shake the feeling of déjà vu.

Connor unlocked the third door on the right and the sensor by the door picked up the movement and turned on the lights. Scattered across the room were numerous stainless steel tables covered with electronics in various stages of assembly. Against the far wall, a specially designed rack held dozens of silver laptops and he went there first.

They were all charged, due Aidan's lengthy absence, so Connor grabbed the first one he found and turned to scan it into the computer, which would activate it.

The level of security utilized by McDougal was astonishing even to a man possessed of Connor's vast knowledge. He often wondered why the man was so intrigued with the ancient past and what it was about his present that made him so neurotically wary. McDougal never accepted visitors and was often compared to Howard Hughes in the latter stages of his dementia.

"Who are you?"

Connor jumped at the sound of McDougal's distinctively raspy voice. He glanced behind him, but he was alone in the room. McDougal was speaking through the crystal-clear speakers positioned in every corner.

"Connor Bruce," he replied, imagining what the man looked like who went with that voice. It sounded almost as if he was on a respirator.

"Should I know you, Mr. Bruce?"

Smiling wryly, Connor shook his head. "No. I'm afraid not, Mr. McDougal."

"Then why are you absconding with my expensive equipment?"

Connor paused in the act of placing the now-functional laptop into its padded case. A reasonable question. And he valued Aidan's job enough to be honest. "Something pressing has come up and I need help."

"Ah, yes. You mercenary types are never completely free of danger are you?"

"You're taking this well," Connor noted.

"How does Mr. Cross figure into this plan of yours?"

"I brained him and stole his car and keys."

"And you magically know your way around my facility as if you've been here many times?"

"Uh. . . something like that."

There was a long hesitation, but Connor kept moving, gathering up all the many items he'd need to track Rachel's cellular signal. "I'm a very wealthy man, Mr. Bruce."

"Yes, sir. I know that." He caught up the bag and left the room, moving with bold strides down the hall.

"There is a good reason for that."

"I'm sure there is." Connor keyed in the code that opened the armory door.

"I don't allow people to take advantage of me."

The lock mechanism beeped its approval and the pneumatic locks disengaged with a sharp hiss. Connor pushed the heavy door open and set his bag down on the table in the center of the room. A marksman's paradise.

"I'm not taking advantage of you, sir." He began pulling handguns from their respective racks and laid them out next to the laptop. "I promise to return everything I'm taking with me today."

"Including Mr. Cross?"

"Especially Cross," Connor said, filling the magazine tube with rounds. "He'll have a nasty bump on the head, but otherwise, he'll be no worse for wear."

"I'm inclined to stop you."

"I'm inclined to make it difficult for you to do so."

"I have a dozen armed men surrounding Cross's vehicle as we speak."

Connor reached behind him and tapped the hilt of his glaive over his shoulder.

"Hmm . . . I have a fondness for swords," McDougal said.

"Me, too. I can kick a lot of ass with one. It's not pretty, so I'd prefer to take a more peaceable route, if you don't mind." Working industriously, Connor dumped out another box of rounds and filled more mag clips.

"You know your way around an armory, Mr. Bruce."

"It's a prerequisite for us mercenary types."

"I could use more men like you," McDougal said, though in truth it was a demand. They both knew Aidan was at his mercy. "I think you owe me for my cooperation, don't you agree?"

"What do you want?"

"A credit for a future task. Of my choosing."

Connor paused and stared grimly down at the weapons in his hands. His instincts were finely honed and he trusted them implicitly. Right now they were clanging hell-for-leather. He exhaled harshly. "Cross keeps his job?"

"Certainly. After all, it's not his fault you brained him, right?"

"Right."

"Excellent!" Satisfaction dripped from the coarse voice. "Puts me in a good mood. Perhaps you could use some assistance? Some manpower? Equipment?"

Oh yeah . . . he was in deep shit if McDougal anticipated his "credit" being worth all that. But what the hell. If he was going to strike a bargain with the devil, he damn well expected to get his soul's worth out of it.

"All of the above," he said, getting back to work. "Can I get a chopper, too?"

Aidan stared down at the somewhat tiny filigreed triangle with its intricate design and wondered what value it held. It was thin, about two inches in diameter with no back to it. He could see right through it, so there was no compartment to hide anything inside. In fact, if he found this without having any preconceived notions of what it was, he'd guess it was a necklace charm or some other bit of jewelry.

"Hey." Lyssa pulled out the chair beside him and sat, setting a cup of steaming coffee down in front of her. "Is that it?"

He shrugged and twisted the book around so that she could see the rendering that had been made of it in the pages. "It's definitely one of the items I was hoping to find, but there are pieces that work in conjunction with it and we don't have them."

"At least it's a triangle," she offered. "That's a good sign."

"Yes, it's hopeful. There's a mention of the Mojave Desert. The coordinates here—" he pointed to the page "—line up to that area and the mentions of caverns seem to confirm it."

She reached out and set her hand over his. "I'm worried. If something happens to Justin, I don't think Stacey can take it. He's all she has."

"I know." He straightened in the chair. "The Elders are very good at finding weaknesses and exploiting them. I anticipated something like this. I just wasn't prepared for them to strike against Stacey."

"How could any of us know?"

"Connor suggested that she might be vulnerable because of how close she is to you. I thought he was bullshitting me, using it as a way to excuse his interest in her. Obviously, I was wrong."

"I think he really likes her."

"Yeah." Aidan heaved out his breath. "I think so, too."

"So where do we go from here?" She released him and sat back.

"I'm going to have to search for more things like this—" he held up the filigreed triangle, "—using a book written when the landscape was totally different than the way it is now. I'll be gone more often than not. If Connor and Stacey can work things out after whatever happens tonight, I'll feel better all around. I can't protect everyone alone, Lyssa. The shit just keeps on coming."

"I'm not sure that his help will be enough, as much as I value it."

"True." Aidan's mouth thinned grimly. "We need reinforcements. As soon as we can catch our breath, Connor is going to have to sit down and figure out who is best to bring over from the Twilight. I haven't been with the men since they've become rebels. I have no idea who is up for the task and who isn't."

Lyssa leaned over and pressed a kiss to his cheek. "I can't believe all the sacrifices the Guardians are making for us."

"It was our fuck-up, Hot Stuff." He cupped the back of her neck and nuzzled his nose against hers. "It's our responsibility to clean it up."

The sound of a car pulling into the drive caught both their attentions. Then another car. And another. Pushing to their feet, they ran to the front door. Stacey stood on the porch, watching the invasion with a blank stare.

A fleet of cars flooded Stacey's property. Hummers, Magnums, Jeeps, and vans, their headlights angled in every direction as they covered the lawn in a broad pattern.

"Holy shit," Lyssa said.

"I'm insane," Stacey muttered, her hands on her sweats-clad hips. "There is no other explanation for this madness."

Connor hopped out of the nearest car, a black Magnum. He caught Aidan's eye and shrugged. "I brought reinforcements."

"I'll say."

The yard was reclaimed by the darkness as headlights were extinguished one by one. Men and women began to climb from their vehicles. Cargo doors and trunks were opened and masses of equipment brought out.

Sprinting up the steps, Connor gestured everyone into the house. "Your home is going to be headquarters, Stace," he explained, holding the door open for her and Lyssa to enter. "There's a transponder in Rachel's cell phone that is sending its location to a receiver on her end. By setting up shop here, it'll appear as if we're staying put."

"Do whatever you want to the damn house," she said, green eyes hard and determined. "As long as I get Justin back, I don't give a shit about anything else."

The screen door was pulled open and a flood of urban camouflaged individuals poured in.

"First," Connor said to the group at large, pointing to Tommy. "Tranq him so he stays knocked out." He looked at Stacey. "We'll take him back to the hotel. Can you write a note saying that Justin called you and complained of homesickness? Make up something about not wanting to get in a fight about it, so you came and left without waking him."

Stacey arched a brow.

"It's as close to plausible as we're going to get on such short notice," Connor argued. "If you've got a better idea, let's hear it."

"Fuck it."

"Right." Connor glanced at Aidan. "Well?"

"It's triangular," Aidan replied, "but it's a small part of a larger whole and until I figure out what the other pieces are, I can't figure out what the purpose is."

Connor caught the bag thrown at him by one of Mc-Dougal's men. "I've got to change into the latest fashion on display here." He gestured at the black, white, and gray-clad people around them. "McDougal didn't have much of a selection in the sportswear department."

"How the hell did you get away with all of this?" Aidan asked.

"A favor of some sort or another."

"I've got your back," Aidan said.

"Thanks. I've got to change before Rachel calls. Hopefully, we can get a beat on her location."

Connor traversed the hall to the guest bathroom, which was decorated in soft sea foam green. Stacey liked color because she had a colorful personality. As he stepped into the shower, he thought of this, thought about how he considered such things about her.

There was a Guardian in the Twilight named Morgan who had been something of a "booty call" to him for centuries. If he wanted a quick fuck with no expectations and even less conversation, she was his girl. Still, despite how often he'd slept with her, Connor couldn't recall what the interior of her home was like. He knew she liked flowers and he always brought her some, but he didn't know what her favorite flower was or what her favorite color was.

He wanted to know everything about Stacey.

Why her? Why now?

"Aw, fuck it!" he muttered, scrubbed out the soap in his hair. His brain hurt from trying to comprehend his feelings.

He cared. Period. Why the hell did he need to know why? He just did.

When Connor exited the steamy bathroom a few minutes later, he found the living room, breakfast nook, and kitchen completely commandeered.

The industrious hum of conversations died suddenly. He frowned, then the soft trill of an uninspired cell phone ring explained the ensuing silence. He jogged to the threshold between the living room and kitchen. Aidan tossed him the phone when he came into view.

Connor caught and flipped it open in one easy movement. "Yes?"

A cord connected the phone to the laptop on the table, which was monitored by a young lady with severely restrained brown hair and an emotionless expression. She gave the thumbs up signal that the trace was in progress.

"*Captain Bruce,*" Rachel purred, "*do you have the trinity?*"

"Gold scrollwork triangle?" he queried. "I've got it."

"*Excellent, after it is safely in my possession, I will send someone--*"

"No way." His grip on the handset tightened. "Even trade. I see the boy alive, you see the trinity."

"*You wound me, Captain. After all we have been through together, you still do not trust me?*"

"Nope. Not a bit."

"Very well, then. Meet me in the parking lot of the Del Mar Mall in Monterey."

"Got it." He glanced at the gal on the laptop. She shook her head.

Damn it, he had to keep her on the line a little longer . . .

"Rachel? A word of advice? Not a scratch on the boy." His voice lowered ominously. "You won't like what happens otherwise."

Connor's teeth grit as Rachel laughed, but he waited for her to disconnect the line before hanging up.

"According to the last tower position, that call didn't come from the north," the brunette said. "It came from the Barstow area."

Aidan glanced at Connor. "I think she's headed to Mojave."

"Can we go now?" Stacey asked, stepping into view from the kitchen.

She was wearing a black ribbed tank top, urban camouflage pants, and jungle boots. More important than that, however, was her expression. Burning eyes and pursed lips told Connor that dissuading her from tagging along was going to be a bitch. "Why don't you help Aidan figure things out?" he suggested.

"Nice try," she retorted. "But I'm not staying here."

He looked back at Aidan. "Are you sending someone up to Monterey?"

They knew each other so well, they could communicate without words. The chances of Rachel separating from her bargaining chip were so slim, they didn't even signify.

Justin was with her. Monterey was a decoy. Since it would take three hours to get to Mojave and several to get to Monterey, she was stalling for time.

"I'm not an idiot," Stacey said, coming over to him. The top of her head barely reached his shoulder, but she set her hands on her hips and looked ready to take him on anyway. "You think you can send me along to Monterey, don't you? It's faster to Mojave and you're hoping that you'll wrap this all up before I'm in danger."

Connor struggled to keep his face stern when he really wanted to smile. "If Justin's in Monterey, that's where you'll want to be."

"Listen." Her head tilted to the side. "I'm going with *you*. If you're going to Monterey, that's where I'm going. If you're going to Mojave, that's where I'm going. Now grab your shit and let's go."

Stacey glanced at Aidan. "Which car are we taking?"

"Stace, please," Lyssa begged. Standing from her seat at the end of the small table. "Stay with me."

"Sorry, Doc. No can do."

Grabbing her arm, Connor led her out through the crowded living room and then outside. He took her to the far corner of the porch, by the bedroom window, as far away as possible from the steady foot traffic moving in and out of the house.

Stacey followed Connor with shaking legs. She hoped he didn't notice how unsteady her steps were. She was terrified he would find a way to leave her behind. Maybe it was unreasonable to feel like she had to be with him, but she couldn't shake the feeling. Her home was no longer her own, Lyssa was a walking guilt-trip, and Aidan was focused on keeping everything running smoothly. She felt like an outsider. Lost, confused, and really goddamned scared.

Connor was her only anchor in the mess that was her life. He was stoic, prepared. Ready to go. What would she do if he left her behind?

He drew to a stop and heaved out a breath. The roof of the porch hid him in shadow, but his eyes glittered with emotions she both longed for and resented.

"Stacey," he began in that low, rich brogue she adored. "What can I do to get you to stay behind?"

"Nothing." Her voice came out hoarser than she would have liked.

"Sweetheart." The aching note in his voice made her cry.

"You can't leave me here, Connor. You can't."

He cupped her face in his hands and pressed firm lips to her brow. "I won't be able to think if you're with me. I'd be too scared for you."

"Please," she begged in scarcely more than a whisper. "Please take me with you. I'll go crazy here."

He was going to say no, she could tell. Her hands fisted in his T-shirt. His skin was so hot she could feel the humidity through the black cotton. "You owe me," she said. "I swear to God I'll never forgive you if you leave me behind. We'll never have a chance -- you and me -- if you go without me."

Tension gripped his frame and his head lifted. "Do we have a chance now?"

She swallowed hard, her chest compressed in a vice of misery and yearning.

"Stacey?" He pressed his parted lips to hers, his tongue flickering along the seam.

"I don't know," she breathed against his mouth. "I can't think about everything now. What you are . . . what this means . . . But I need you. I need to be with you."

Connor nuzzled his temple against hers and cursed under his breath. "You have to listen to me. Obey every command without question."

"Yes," she promised, surging into him. "Yes, whatever you say."

"You'll be the death of me," he murmured, taking her mouth with deep, possessive licks. His thumbs brushed across her cheekbones, wiping at the wetness left by her tears. His grip was almost too tight, his passion almost too much.

She welcomed it, welcomed his warmth and strength when she had none, and she missed it when he pulled away reluctantly.

"Let's grab our bags," he said with a resigned sigh. "The sooner we take off, the sooner we'll have Justin back."

Filled with gratitude, she restrained him and kissed him one more time. "Thank you."

"I don't like this," he growled. "I don't like it at all."

But he was doing it anyway, because he couldn't deny her. There was something precious in that capitulation.

Stacey stored away the feeling to examine another day.

Chapter 14

Connor stared straight down the highway and wondered at his sanity. It was shot to hell apparently; otherwise Stacey would not be in the passenger seat next to him.

"So all of your people are immortal?" she asked tentatively.

His grip on the steering wheel tightened. The powerful HEMI engine of the Magnum hurtled them along Interstate 15 at eighty-five miles per hour, but the restlessness eating at him made it feel like they were standing still. They weren't reaching their destination fast enough.

"We can be killed," he said finally, "but it takes a lot of work."

"Are you going to k-kill Rachel?"

He shot a side-glance at her. "I may have to."

She nodded grimly.

"I'll do everything I can to keep this neat and clean, but if it comes down to the wire, we can't afford to fail."

"No, we can't." She offered him a shaky smile that was

meant to be reassuring and his heart clenched. "I figured you might need me when you handed me this gun and started explaining."

"That's to protect yourself. Don't worry about me, Stacey." He reached out and set his hand over hers where it held the Glock. "Keep yourself alive. That's the most important thing."

The silence stretched out between them. Not quite comfortable, not quite uncomfortable.

She blew out her breath, then twisted in the seat to face him. "So I hold both arms out steady, and just keep pulling the trigger until all the bullets are gone. Even if they're down for the count?"

"Yeah, especially if they're down. You can't kill them with a gun. You can only slow them down long enough for me to finish the job."

"With the sword."

"That's right. Guardians can heal most injuries, but we can't grow back limbs or our heads."

"Yuck." She shuddered.

"And keep your eyes open. Sounds obvious, I know, but the report of the gun naturally causes the eyes to blink. You can fuck up a shot that way."

"Eyes open. Okay."

The hands-free communications system signaled an incoming call and they glanced at each other. Connor activated the line and said, "Tell me you have something good, Cross."

Aidan's brogue came through the speakers. "We've got a location on the black sedan. Your recollection of the plate numbers was right on and that led us to a rental agency in

San Diego who has GPS locators on all of their vehicles. You're almost on top of them now."

"Where?" Stacey cried.

"They stopped in Barstow, near where the trace lost the cellular signal. Hopefully, they decided to hole up for the night and didn't just ditch the car."

Connor looked at the green highway sign they passed. "We'll be in Barstow in just a few minutes."

"I've got a chopper on the way," Aidan said. "We may need it."

"Stace?" Lyssa's voice come over the line filled with concern. "How are you doing?"

"I'm okay, Doc."

"The crew here is in raptures over your pie," Lyssa said. "I hope you don't mind. It's been a few hours since you left and they're getting hungry."

"Are you kidding?" Stacey smiled wryly. "They're helping me get my kid back. I love each and every one of them. They can eat whatever they want."

"Hey!" Connor complained, working with Lyssa to keep Stacey's spirits up. "Save me a slice."

"Don't worry." Stacey touched his forearm, then pulled away quickly. "I'll make you your own pie. You won't have to share."

The look she gave him made his breath catch. There was affection there. Her body language told him she was wary, but her overture gave him hope.

"They're fighting over who can have some," Lyssa said with a soft laugh. "Too many people, not enough pie."

"It's still not better than sex," Aidan insisted.

"Depends on the sex," someone shouted out in the background.

That brought a genuine smile to Stacey's face. It did Connor's heart good to see some life in her. She was so pale, her eyes so big, her lush mouth framed by deep grooves of stress.

"You guys are making me hungry," he complained. He hadn't eaten since breakfast, which was not the way he liked to go into battle.

"Okay." The alertness in Aidan's tone caught Connor's attention. "You're going to take your next exit."

Glancing over his shoulder, Connor was grateful for both the number of dreams he'd shared where he learned to drive and also for the light traffic. Pretty much the only vehicles behind them were reinforcements—vans with cleanup crews and Hummers with armed backup. One day, he'd ask Aidan why McDougal needed a personal army, but right now, he was grateful for the support. "Okay, we're on the off ramp."

Aidan directed them away from the freeway to a motel that had probably never had a good day to begin with, and certainly wasn't having one now. The two-story building appeared to have once been painted peach and brown, but in the yellow glow of the parking lot lights it was hard to tell for sure. The paint was cracked and peeling, the colors faded by the California sun.

Connor parked the car a short distance up the road from the establishment and said, "We're going in."

"Be careful," Aidan admonished. "I know you've never worked with humans before, so listen to me: Don't try and do everything yourself. McDougal is a savvy spender. He only hires the best. Trust your team to do their job. I'm fairly confident that you're going to pay through the nose for their help, so use it. I need you alive."

"Got it." While the order was given bluntly, Connor understood the friendship behind the words and took comfort in it. He was in a strange world, but he wasn't as alone as he'd first felt.

Disconnecting the line, he climbed out of the car and looked over the roof at Stacey as she did the same. His shoulders were well above the roofline. She was height-challenged, lifting to her tiptoes to see him more comfortably.

"Here's how we are going to handle this," he began. "We're just going to have a look around. Check out the car and the front desk. See if they're here or if they switched transportation and bailed."

She nodded grimly.

"Don't try to be a hero," she said. "I'm good, sweetheart, believe me. But with multiple opponents and a hostage at stake, I'm not in a position to fight them all and keep an eye on you. If they're here, you need to stay out of harm's way so I can concentrate on getting Justin back, not saving your ass."

He saw how much that killed her. The thought that her son could be close and she might have to restrain herself. Still, she said, "I understand."

"Do you trust me?" He made no effort to hide the emotions behind the question. Right now, his lack of detachment was both his greatest strength and his biggest liability.

Stacey's lips compressed until they were white, then tears glistened in her eyes.

Connor slammed his palm down on the roof so hard he startled her, making her gasp and jump.

"Damn it! Stop thinking about all the losers in your past and think about *me!* Do you trust *me?*"

"We just fucking met!" she hissed back at him. "Don't act like we've known each other forever."

"I care about you, Stacey. It doesn't matter how long we've known each other or not. It comes from here," he hit his chest, "and it's important to me. I think if you stopped trying to convince yourself that all men are the same, you'd realize that time doesn't matter."

"Easy for you to say, Mr. My-life-is-endless."

"Yeah, and your life isn't and you're wasting it." Connor held up a hand to cut her off. "I've lived centuries, Stacey. I've known a lot of women. I've spent years with some. I've done things with them that I haven't had time yet to do with you, but I already know this is different."

Shaking his head, he backed up and opened the rear driver's side door. "Forget it. I don't know why I asked."

"I didn't say I don't trust you." She came around the back of the car.

"You didn't say you did either."

He motioned her closer and then held up a shoulder holster for her to maneuver into. "You're going to wear this to hold the gun. If you have to, defend yourself." He tightened the straps until it was snugly secured, then he turned her to face him. "But I want you to run first. Shoot only if you have no other choice. Got it?"

"Yes."

Connor moved to turn away and she caught his arm. "I don't think you're like any other guy I've ever known." Her thumb stroked over his skin restlessly, an innocent absentminded caress.

"Damn fucking right I'm not," he growled, kissing her hard and swift before she could pull away. "I'm the guy who's going to wear you down. The guy who's going to make a nuisance of himself every time he's in town. The guy who's going to seduce you every chance he gets, even when you say no . . . Shit, especially when you say no."

Stacey gazed up at him with wide eyes and worried her lower lip.

"I can't promise to wear a suit and come home for dinner every night." He pushed her away and reached into the backseat for his scabbard, which he slung over his back. "But I can promise to care about you. And I'm stubborn, so get used to me."

Grabbing a windbreaker, he shoved it at her. "That'll help to hide the guns." Then he looked down at himself and groaned. "Okay. We look like hoodlums. Fuck."

"This is where I come in handy." Stacey reached into her pockets and pulled out a pair of colorful sparkling rubber bands. Within minutes she had two childish pigtails sticking out the top of her head and garish red lipstick on her mouth. She used the reflection of the car window to secure a leather collar to her neck, then faced him. "Ta da!"

Connor's brows rose. "Yikes."

She shrugged. "I figured these pants were going to take some creativity to pull off, so I came prepared to look weird enough to wear them. There's nothing I can do about your sword though or the goon squad." Stacey gestured to the small army getting ready just a few feet away. "We'll just have to play it like we're looking for a costume party, if someone asks."

"Right . . . well . . . I like the collar."

Stacey shivered under the intense appreciation she saw in Connor's gaze. Even pissed off, frustrated, and under a great deal of stress he still tried to compliment her. Regardless of the situation between them, she loved him for that and for caring enough about her to go through all of this. Sure, his "people" had a vested interest in what was going on. But he was fighting for Justin more than he was fighting over the trinity. She knew that for a fact.

"Are we ready?" she asked, the words husky with gratitude.

"As we'll ever be." He shut the door and gripped her by the elbow. Connor looked at the men waiting nearby and said, "Four of you check the perimeter. The rest come with me."

As he led her away there was strength and command in his touch, and Stacey appreciated both as they crossed the street and entered the parking lot of the motel. The pavement was cracked and worn, the cars in the spaces bearing more-than-average wear and tear. Many of the lights were either out or flickering with an annoying high-volume humming that grated on Stacey's already raw nerves. Litter spoiled on the ground and in the near distance, a dog howled plaintively, an apt accompaniment to such squalor.

They had a dozen men with them total. Of the eight who stayed close, four branched off at Connor's gestured command and began weaving through the parked cars.

"You know," Stacey began. "I just can't see Rachel stopping for the night in a place like this. Not when there are tons of other lodgings here in town and Mojave is so close."

Out of the corner of her eye, she saw him nod. "I agree. They probably ditched the car, but even that's odd. Talk about sticking out like a sore thumb. Look at it. You can't miss it."

The cloud-filtered moonlight glimmered off the black paint, which made finding the sedan easy, despite its location in an unlit corner of the lot. They approached it slowly, cautiously. Connor took the lead; she followed a few steps behind with the others.

He paused several feet away and gestured to the nearby thick cement base that supported one of the lamps. "Wait over there and help look out."

"What am I looking out for?" she asked.

"Anyone coming by." His gaze was hard and fierce as he looked at one of the men in a nonverbal communication that was beyond her. "I need a closer look at that car and I don't want to be disturbed. Check your sides often and listen for any suspicious noises."

She was pretty sure he was just trying to get her out of his hair, but she'd promised to listen and she would.

Without another word, Stacey did as he asked, following the guy assigned to her to the requested position. Her gaze roamed the lot in a steady back-and-forth sweep. The lamp she stood under was dead center at the end, which afforded her an open view of the property. It also offered a hideous smell. It was her guess that more than a few animals—and perhaps even humans—had used the distant location as a urinal.

Her stomach roiled with a mixture of disgust and fear. Connor and the others worked almost silently, doing whatever the hell it was that they were doing to the car. The guy next to her said nothing and bore no expression at all on his face or in his eyes.

The temperature was chilly, but Stacey suspected it was her own fear that made her shiver so violently. The neon vacancy sign blinked off and on, coaxing her to stare briefly at the glass door to the front desk. That was as dirty as the rest of the place. Spattered with something foul and so grimy it obviously hadn't been washed in years.

Connor returned to her with such stealth Stacey wouldn't have been aware of him if she hadn't been keeping vigil. She raised her brows in query.

"Let's go to the office," he said with alarming alacrity, snatching her elbow and dragging her away.

"Why?"

"Because I said."

There was something underlying his tone that made her look back over her shoulder. Two of the men remained with the vehicle in defensive positions. She couldn't see what they'd done to the sedan, if anything.

Then a flash of glimmered moonlight caught her eye. She slowed.

Something was dripping from the trunk onto the asphalt, forming an ever-growing puddle. From the rate of seepage, the substance was thicker than water. . .

"Oh my god!" She stumbled and Connor kept her upright, his pace unchanged. "What's in the trunk?"

"Our friend with the teeth."

Her heart dropped into her stomach and she swallowed

hard. "You thought Justin might be in there, didn't you? That's why you made me move away."

"It was a possibility."

His jaw was locked, his eyes forward, his step purpose-ful.

"You think he's dead, don't you?" Her voice rose and she fought his grip. "What did you see in there? Tell me!"

Connor halted and yanked her into him. "Keep your voice down, damn it!"

He gestured the other men onward with a quick jerk of his chin. When they were alone, he said, "There's nothing in there but a head and a body, neither of which belong to your son."

"Oh my god . . . oh my god . . ."

"This is where that trust I asked for comes into play."

Nodding violently, she pulled away to fight the feeling of claustrophobia.

"Stace." His brogue softened. "We're going to the office now. We need to disable any security cameras this sorry assed place might have and find out which of the rooms are presently occupied. Then we're going door to door until we're sure they're not here."

Stacey bent over, gasping. As cold as she'd been a moment ago, she was sweating now. "You don't think they left?"

"They probably did, but we have to be sure. Come on." He tugged her up and kept going. "You wanted to come; you have to keep it together."

How was she going to keep it together when she felt like vomiting? The people who had her son were the type of in-dividuals who decapitated others and stuffed their bodies in trunks. "I feel sick."

He cursed under his breath and stopped again. "Don't do this to me," he said brusquely. "I've got to keep going. Do you understand that? I promised you I would get Justin back. I promised you that if you gave me a chance, I would deliver. Don't make me fail."

Gasping for air, she nodded, clearing her mind of terrifying images by sheer will alone. He was right. She knew he was right. She'd fuck everything up if she lost it now. "I'm with you."

Connor pulled her upright and tilted her chin skyward, opening her airways to facilitate deep breaths. "You're brave, sweetheart." He kissed the tip of her nose. "I'm proud of you. Now, let's go."

One foot in front of the other. Stacey knew she could make it in baby steps. At least she thought so until they reached the door to the office and one of the men intercepted them.

"You might want to keep the lady out, sir," he said.

It was then Stacey realized the dirt splattered on the glass was blood. And that was only a miniscule amount of the volume of gore that covered what she could see of the front desk area.

She gagged.

"You can't throw up," Connor growled, clamping a hand over her mouth and dragging her away. His voice came low and rough by her ear. "The authorities are going to investigate this. You can't leave any biological evidence behind. You understand? Nod, if you understand."

Stacey couldn't move. She was frozen in place by the horror of what she'd seen.

"Okay." He picked her up and moved her out to the

public curb. "Let's get you back to the car. We'll lock you in. You keep the gun at the ready . . ."

Struggling, she managed to get him to set her down. "I can do this," she promised. "I can help you."

"You're a wreck," he said. "You're going to get yourself arrested and charged with murder."

"I'll be your lookout." Stacey watched him shake his head. Setting her hand on his chest, she said, "I'll never forgive myself if I don't help you."

"You can help me by calling Aidan back and bringing him up to speed." Connor cupped her face and stared down into her eyes. The emotion in the liquid depths was visible even in the darkness. "You are a precious, cheery light in my life. I want to keep you that way. Let me protect you from this much, at least."

She considered that a moment, but couldn't fight the feeling she was letting him down. Then she glanced over his shoulder at the front desk and her stomach churned violently.

"Yeah, you're right," she admitted. "I can't take it. Take me back to the car. I'll make the phone call."

Connor put his hand at the small of her back and directed her toward the Magnum with strides so long she had to jog to keep up.

"I'm sorry," she said, as he unlocked the door with the remote and assisted her into the passenger seat.

"For what? For doing the right thing? For knowing your limits?" He bent down and looked her in the eye. "I admire you, sweetheart. I'm not disappointed."

Straightening, he said, "I'll be back. Keep the gun ready in your lap. Call Aidan."

He shut the door and reactivated the alarm system with the remote. And then he was gone.

Stacey ignored the hands-free system in favor of direct use of the handset. Aidan answered immediately. "What have you got?"

"Hey, it's me."

Aidan's voice softened. "Hey, Stace. What's going on?"

"We found the car. The driver's dead. Decapitated in the trunk. Someone's dead in the office. Or multiple some-ones. I couldn't go in. There's so much blood. T-tons of it. Ev-verywhere—"

"Shh, it's okay. We'll take care of it. How are you hold-ing up? You doing alright?"

"Yeah." She blew out her breath and glanced toward the lobby.

"Where's Connor?"

"He went to see which rooms are occupied."

The office was located on the corner created by the driveway and the road. Two solid walls of the lobby were glass, providing a view to the interior from the street and also from the motel itself. Various brochure stands and a cloth-draped table with a coffeemaker atop it blocked the lower view to the inside. As she watched, Connor spoke to one of the men, who nodded in reply and then headed toward her.

"Where are you?"

"He locked me in the car."

"Good. Sit tight. There are others on the way. They'll be there shortly."

"C-Connor—" Her voice broke.

"Don't worry about him," Aidan said firmly. "I've fought

beside him a long time, Stace. He's the best soldier I know. If it were my child, I wouldn't choose anyone but him to help me. He's just that damn good."

She gave a jerky nod.

"Stace? You okay?"

"Yes. Sorry. I forgot you can't see me." A crazed little laugh escaped her. "I can't believe this afternoon I was baking a pie." *And making love with a man who makes me weak in the knees.*

"Hang in there. Once we get the motel secured, you can ride the chopper back."

Shaking her head, she said, "No. I have to be there when they find Justin."

Aidan's sigh was audible. "Keep listening to Connor, then."

"Of course."

They disconnected. Stacey was left with a heavy silence and a guard by her door. She realized that her heart was racing madly and her breathing was shallow, both reactions were making her lightheaded.

"Jesus," she muttered, forcing herself to breathe slow and easy. "Get a grip, Stace."

A glimmer of light caught her eye.

Already on edge, her head swiveled to the left where the edge of the road met a slight embankment spotted with trees.

Rachel stood there with a horror of a grin, her once-beautiful face a nightmare of scratches and gouges that would have killed a human. She was missing a chunk of her scalp, the flesh torn so deeply bone was visible.

But that wasn't what caused Stacey to scream.

The full measure of her terror was for her son, who hung limp and unconscious in one of Rachel's arms. The woman's other hand was occupied by a wicked looking sword.

The guard, alerted by her piercing cries, spotted the macabre pair. Yelling into his headset, he charged in their direction. Stacey struggled with the door, feeling frantically for the lock, cursing in frustration until the damn thing gave way and freed her. Stumbling out, she gasped as Connor flew past. She attempted to follow, stepping around the bumper only to gag violently.

The guard's decapitated head rolled to a halt at her feet, his sightless eyes and gaping mouth forever frozen in terror.

Looking up, she saw at least a half dozen of the grinning, ghoulish creatures descending on Connor in a swarm. His blade glinted and flashed with extraordinary speed, his two-fisted swinging dismembering limbs left and right. He fought in a moving circle of steel, spinning and arching in a fatal dance. More camouflaged guards ran up the short rise, creating a scene straight out of a horror flick.

Stacey took in the awesome display in a daze, marveling at the grace and power with which Connor moved. He was so big, yet his agility and speed were impressive. It gave her confidence to see him engaged with such skill and focus. Without him, she was certain she'd be paralyzed with fear. With him, she felt capable of anything.

Taking off at a run, Stacey thrust her right hand into her windbreaker and wrapped it around the grip of the Glock. She yanked it free and took comfort in its weight. She'd never fired a gun in her life, but she was more than ready to shoot the hell out of something now.

Stumbling over a tree root, Stacey fell to her knees in a jarring, painful impact. She lumbered to her feet and pressed onward, but the brief delay was fortuitous. It slowed her down, affording her the time to spot the sole of a shoe beside a tree to her right.

Justin's shoe.

Stacey ran toward it. Picked it up. Looked beyond it. Saw the other.

That one was still attached to her son.

"Justin!" She scrambled over to him, her free hand feeling along his body for injuries. For signs of life. He was so pale, his eyes so bruised looking, the side of his face caked with dried blood spatter. She set the gun down and shook his shoulders. "Justin! Baby, wake up. Wake up, baby, please! Justin!"

She thumped his chest and slapped his cheeks. "Baby. Baby, don't do this to me. You wake up! *Justin!*"

He coughed and Stacey cried out in relief, her vision blurring with tears, her heart aching as he curled up on his side and groaned. She was so focused on him she failed to see the approaching danger until it was too late. A sharp, deep pain struck her arm, then an icy chill spread through the muscle. She screamed and flailed wildly.

A feral, masculine roar filled the air. There was a brief glimpse of golden hair, then Rachel was yanked upwards and tossed away as if she weighed nothing. The damaged woman rolled away with a gurgling laugh, leaving Stacey to find the massive syringe that hung from where it pierced her biceps.

"I will return for what is inside you," the woman hissed,

leaping to safety with preternatural strength when Connor lunged his blade first after her.

"You fucking bitch!" Stacey screamed, reaching for the gun and falling to her back.

Connor tackled Rachel and twisted along the ground with her. Stacey struggled for a clean shot, but as the unbearable chill moved up her arm and into her brain, she knew she was going to pass out.

Just as blackness began to narrow her vision, Rachel reared up and provided a perfect target. Aiming between her spread legs, Stacey fired one round after another, emptying the clip into Rachel's brutalized body. The woman jerked with each impact, then fell to the ground.

Laughing.

As Stacey lost consciousness, that laugh followed her into oblivion.

Chapter 15

"How are you doing, champ?" Connor asked, as he settled onto Stacey's couch next to Justin and handed him an oversized mug of hot chocolate.

"I'm freezing." Dark shadows rimmed the boy's dilated eyes and his skin bore unhealthy pallor—signs of shock. A lock of brown hair fell over his brow, making him appear lost and far younger than his fourteen years.

"I'll get you another blanket."

The front door was open, making the chill worse, but McDougal's men were still clearing out and Justin didn't want to go to his room. He preferred the heavy foot traffic and the drone of the ignored television, because it made him feel safe to be surrounded by so many people.

"Thanks, Connor."

The gratitude on Justin's face hit Connor hard. The Elders would pay for what happened tonight. Dearly.

"You're welcome."

Pushing to his feet, Connor moved toward the hallway

and Justin's room. The boy had been given a dose of propranolol in the chopper and he would continue to take the medication four times a day for the next ten days. The "pill to forget" was still experimental, but clinical trials offered hopeful results and Connor had his fingers crossed the drug would work its magic on Justin.

The boy would still remember the events, but the emotions behind the memories would not be there. His recollections would be detached from his feelings, making him an objective observer more so than an emotionally scarred victim. Healers in the Twilight would help with the rest.

Connor was just opening the bedroom door when Aidan stepped out of Stacey's bedroom. "How's she doing?" he asked, his gut tightening.

"She's stable, although still unconscious." Aidan stepped closer. "There's something in her brain, Bruce. It's small—about the size of a grain of rice—but it's foreign. There's no telling how her body will react to it over time."

Reaching a hand out, Connor braced his weight against the wall and sucked in a deep breath. "Fuck . . . man." He gazed at his friend helplessly. "Do we know what it is?"

"She's talking in her sleep—" Aidan winced, "—in the language of the Ancients."

"*What?*" Running a hand through his hair, Connor groaned. "How do we get it out of her head?"

"Medically, we can't. Not here in this plane, not without killing her. Humans don't have the technology."

The door to the bedroom opened and a man peaked out. "She's conscious."

Connor straightened. "Can I tell her son? Can he see her?"

"She's lucid," the man said.

"Tell her I'll be there in a minute, okay?" Connor looked Aidan. "I have to get Justin."

Aidan nodded and Connor hurried back to the living room.

"Hey," he said, nearing the sofa. "Your mom's awake."

"Can I see her?" Justin sat up from his reclined position and set his half-empty mug on the coffee table.

"Yeah, come on." Connor helped dig him out from under the three or four blankets he had on and walked with him back to Stacey's room.

They entered the darkened space as quietly as possible. Beside the bed, various monitors beeped and flashed with lights. Stacey lay bundled in the middle, a tiny, fragile form that made Connor's chest tighten.

"Hi, baby," she whispered to Justin, holding out her arms to him. Justin immediately climbed up beside her and began sobbing. Stacey joined him, wrapping her arms around her son and pressing her teary cheek to the top of his head.

The sight made Connor's eyes sting. He looked away and found Aidan by the door. His friend gestured him over and Connor went, glad to be distracted from the emotion of the scene behind him. Emotion that was killing him inside, twisting through his gut like a knife.

"I spoke with her briefly," Aidan whispered. "She says Rachel intends to return for that thing in her head. Whatever it is, they think it's safer with us than them."

Connor's entire body tensed. "Or else they think we'd destroy it if it weren't inside something we couldn't bear to lose. Tell me McDougal's men found Rachel."

"They didn't." Aidan's countenance was grave. "They've been searching the area since you left. There's no trace of her. Despite her injuries, she managed to escape."

"Fuck!"

"Watch the language," Stacey admonished.

He turned to look at her. She stared at him with glistening eyes and puckered her lips in a kissing gesture. A low sound of longing rumbled in his throat.

"I don't know what to do," he said, facing Aidan again. "I don't know where I should go, or what I should do, or how I should feel."

"You do what I did," Aidan said. "You forget the 'shoulds' and you jump."

Connor snorted. "Nothing is ever that easy when it comes to women."

"I didn't say it was easy. But if you want her, make it work. It's worth it to be happy."

Happiness. Connor wanted it. He wanted it with Stacey. "Right." And just that quickly, he decided. "So, before McDougal's men totally clear out, let's get a security system out of them. They've got to have top-of-the-line shit. I want this house locked up so tight Ft. Knox will be jealous. I'll be gone a lot. I need to know they're protected."

"Great idea." Aidan smiled, opened the door, and gestured him out first. "Let's get my money's worth."

Stacey woke with a violent, skull-crushing headache.

Both palms pressed flat to her temples, she rolled and writhed, groaning. She bumped into Justin and he mumbled a protest. Whispering an apology, she rolled the other way and fell off the side of her bed. She hit the floor on her knees and cried out, biting her lower lip to stem any more noises. A quick glance at the clock showed it was nearly three in the morning. The way her head felt, she doubted she'd live to see the sunrise.

She crawled a few feet, then rose by necessity. It was too jarring to move on her hands and knees. How she made it down the hall, she'd never know, but it was colder in the open space of the living room and the chill eased the burning of her skin.

"Stacey?"

Connor's deep brogue curled around her spine and coursed down like warm honey. Relief flooded her and nearly brought her to the floor again.

"Where are you?" she gasped, afraid to open her eyes. The moonlight slanting upward to the ceiling from the shutters was too much light even from behind hastily closed lids. The full brunt would only increase the feeling of having an ice pick piercing straight through to her brain.

"Here," he rumbled, "I'm right here."

Warm arms wrapped around her, cradling her to a hard, nude chest lightly dusted with hair.

"I'm so glad you stayed."

"I'm not leaving you, sweetheart. Even when I'm not here, I won't really be gone."

"My head hurts," she whimpered, tears coursing down her cheeks.

"The doctor left some medicine for you. Let me—"

"No!" She clung to his waistband, recognizing by touch that he wore sweats. The thought of him here, sleeping on her couch, protecting her, made her feel loved and safe in a way nothing else in her life ever had. "Don't leave me."

"Sweetheart." His lips pressed to her forehead and some of the pain eased. "It kills me to see you crying."

"Do that again," she begged. "Kiss me again."

His mouth touched her skin, this time against her closed eyes and lashes, kissing away the tears. The throbbing in her head lessened.

Tilting her neck back, Stacey captured his lips with her own. The instant she tasted him, her blood heated and began to flow, her heart rate picked up. Miraculously, the debilitating pressure eased.

"Stace," he mumbled into her mouth as she grew more fervent. "What are you doing?"

"I want you."

She felt the surprise move through him, then the desire he couldn't control.

"You're nuts," he said, but his hands were on her hips, his fingers sliding beneath her cotton shirt to touch the skin of her back. His touch was soothing, calming.

The more he touched her, the less her head hurt.

"Make love to me," she pleaded.

"Justin . . . ?"

"The laundry room has a door."

"You shouldn't—"

"Now, Connor!"

"Aw, fuck." He picked her up and carried her to the back of the house. Stepping into the laundry room, he kicked aside the basket that held the door open and pushed the portal closed. He sat her down atop the old desk she used as a folding table and stared at her with a bemused smile and hot gaze. "Now what?"

In the back of her mind a sharp squealing noise resembled tires burning rubber. "Don't stop touching me."

Setting his hands on either side of her hips, Connor caged her to the desk and nuzzled his lips against her neck. "Tell me what you need, sweetheart."

She reached for him, embraced him. Beneath her palms she felt hot, silken skin stretched over rippling, flexing muscle and she melted inside. She moaned when his teeth nipped her earlobe. "I need you."

"You've got me." He pressed her back onto the desk and his hand slipped between her legs. Even through the thick camouflage, his fingertips had no trouble giving her what she wanted. "I'm not going anywhere. We'll make this work."

"Yes . . . oh that feels good . . ."

"Hmmm," he agreed, deftly freeing the button at her waistband before pulling the zipper down. The whole time his lips, tongue, and teeth were doing something wonderful to the tender skin of her throat and his other hand cushioned the back of her head so that his big, hard body was literally wrapped around hers. The noises in her head fell silent. Or else they were drowned out by the rushing of blood in her ears.

"Connor." Her nostrils filled with his scent. There was no other scent in the world like his—spicy and exotic. Foreign. She loved it. Her very own man of her dreams.

He was right; time didn't matter. What mattered was the way she felt when they were together. He had been a rock of stability when she needed him and she knew he always would be. That was just his way.

She gasped as his hand slipped beneath the waistband of her panties.

"How does your head feel?" His voice was dark as sin, his accent thick and dripping with lust.

"I-I . . ."

"Does your head still hurt?" Connor kissed her with fervent passion, his tongue gliding along hers expertly, taking her mind off everything but him. A rough, edgy growl rumbled in his chest as she grew wet against his fingertips.

"Oh god." Stacey moaned, her eyes clenching shut as he slid a finger inside her. "Fuck me, please! Hurry."

He hushed her frantic cries with his mouth and gently cradled her descent as he laid her flat atop the desk. He tugged her pants down to her knees, lifted her joined legs into air, and set them against his shoulder. When she felt the warm, silky smooth head of his cock, Stacey writhed with hunger, needing him inside her.

"Shh . . . Here you go, sweetheart," he purred.

Her hands wrapped around the curved edges of the desktop as his thick cock pushed into her. She cried out, arching in pleasure. She was tight in this position, forcing him to work his way into her with short, fierce digs.

Mewling with pleasure, she struggled to take all that he had. "You're too big like this," she gasped.

"You'll take me." He rolled his hips and slid deeper. Advancing. Retreating. Claiming her body inch by tortuously good inch.

Her nails dug crescents into the wood as he stroked deeper, massaging the broad head of his cock across that greedy spot inside her that could never get enough of him.

"Stacey," he breathed roughly, pumping his hips. "Your

pussy is so damn tight like this. Like a hot, wet fist. So fucking good. I think I might come before I get all the way inside you."

"Don't you dare!" She cupped her aching breasts and squeezed. "You started this. You better finish."

"Oh, I'll finish." His gorgeous face was flushed, his eyes dark, his forehead misted with sweat. "Fuck . . . yeah . . . I'm going to finish. Deep inside you."

Dear god, would she survive it?

He was working her into a frenzy, thrusting harder and faster. The waistband of his sweats, lowered just to his hips, rubbed against her thighs. The sight was intensely erotic, as was her position, bound and positioned for his pleasure. His hips swiveled and thrust, in and out. Her cunt rippled along his cock, on the verge of orgasm.

Stacey's back arched, her entire body tense and expectant. This was what she needed, what she wanted. To be connected to him, wanted by him. "Yes . . ."

Connor stroked deeper, his heavy testicles slapping rhythmically against the curve of her ass, making her pussy clench tight around him. She watched him with heavy-lidded eyes, taking in his passion-flushed features and the lock of golden hair that fell over his brow. His biceps and pectorals were defined by the effortless hold he had on her. His abdomen flexed as he fucked her, the golden skin glistening with sweat.

"You're mine," he gritted out. "I'm keeping you."

His possessiveness thrilled her, pushing her that last little bit she needed to climax. Stacey bit her lip to keep from crying out as the orgasm tightened her entire body.

Connor grunted and fucked through her spasms,

increasing his pace until she thought she would scream with the pleasure. It was only the nearby door and their need for privacy that forced her to silence.

She felt him swell, grow impossibly harder, and then he groaned, "*Stacey . . .*"

His hips jack hammered against hers, rocking the old desk, his fingers digging into the flesh of her thighs. His cock jerked, then spurted, filling her in a thick rush of heat. He continued to take her, stroking through her clenching pussy, emptying his lust and love at the deepest point of her.

"Fuck," he gasped when it was over, resting his cheek against her calf. "You'll kill me."

"My head doesn't hurt anymore," she said in breathless wonder.

"I can't even feel my head," Connor replied. "I think you blew it off."

She laughed with pure feminine triumph.

Stepping back, Connor withdrew from her body. He dried his cock with a nearby towel and tugged up his sweats, then he took care of cleaning and dressing her.

"Come here, baby." Connor's voice was filled with tenderness as he collected her in his arms.

Stacey held on tight. "I think I'm falling love with you," she admitted shyly. "I hope that doesn't freak you out. I have a tendency to jump into things and with you—"

His lips pressed against hers, halting the spill of words. "Go ahead and jump," he urged hoarsely. "I'll jump with you."

Chapter 16

Philip Wager stared at the data on the screen with wide eyes, his heart thumping in a desperate, frantic tempo. His fingers clung to the edge of the console with white-knuckled force and he forced himself to release his grip. He pushed the chair back and rose to his feet.

"Fuck," he whispered, his brain scrambling to comprehend the information in front of him. "That's impossible."

"Obviously not," murmured a voice behind him.

He spun and faced his visitor, wincing inwardly at the sight of the man who stood there. His glaive was out of reach behind him, leaving him completely vulnerable to the tip of the blade leveled at his chest. "Elder Sheron," he replied, glancing over the gray-robed shoulder to the cavern hallway beyond. He searched for both a means of entry and a source of assistance. Neither was readily visible.

"Wager," Sheron greeted in a conversational tone.

"How did you get in here?"

"I can gain entry to anywhere. I had no part in the building of the Twilight, but every upgrade and enhancement made to the matrix in the last several centuries came from me."

Philip's heart stuttered as he considered the value of such knowledge.

"I can see you appreciate the possibilities." Sheron's voice was filled with a mentor's pride. "Most of the Elders chose to concentrate their attentions on making rules. They believe that is the source of our authority. I, however, knew our true power came from our ability to create the Twilight. Therefore, I wanted to know everything about it. It was considered the least desirable of tasks, so I was free to do as I wished."

"You planted the bug." There were hundreds of questions in Philip's mind, but he knew the answer to that query for a certainty.

"Yes, and I always knew you would be the one who would dig deep enough to find it. I tried to have you eliminated, but the others would not hear of it. They did not know my reasons, you see. They felt denying you advancement was punishment enough for your perceived offenses, which I exaggerated, of course." The Elder waved one hand dismissively. "Since you did not have access to the equipment required to find me out, I let it go. But I was aware that someday it would come to this."

"What are you doing?" Philip asked, backing toward his glaive, which rested in its scabbard atop a table in the corner. "You must have been planning this for centuries."

Sheron reached up and pushed back his cowl, revealing a chilling smile. "Yes. I have. Which is why I cannot allow you to ruin everything. All these eons of biding my time, moving my pieces across the board slowly but surely. Can you imagine how much patience has been required? I am so close now. But you could ruin everything in a moment."

"Explain to me what you're up to," Philip coaxed, still retreating, hoping to get near enough to his glaive to lunge for it and defend himself. "I can help you."

"You assume my motives are altruistic and you would want to help me. Or perhaps you are simply hoping to distract me from noticing how you move toward your weapon."

Philip stilled and shrugged. Sheron laughed.

"If it consoles you any," the Elder said, "your sacrifice will serve the greater good."

"Oh really?" Philip drawled. "And here I thought you just wanted to prevent me from telling anyone you have a half-mortal daughter."

"There is that, too. There are only two people who know, and that is one person too many."

"She is partnered with a Guardian." Perhaps his mind was more devious, but for Philip, the possibilities inherent in that mating were both plentiful and terrifying. "Was that your intent all along?"

Sheron gripped his glaive more securely. "My apologies, lieutenant. Time is of the essence. I must kill you now. I cannot stay and chat."

Philip crouched, prepared.

The Elder thrust forward in a fatal lunge.

Chapter 17

Stacey eased her foot off the gas pedal as her car approached her house, enjoying the view of her family from a distance. Connor stood in the light of the setting sun like a golden god, his bare back glistening with the sweat from his exertions, his powerful biceps flexing as he drilled another screw into the white picket fence that was quickly replacing her old chain link.

From the moment the realtor had shown her the house, she'd thought its quaint charm was lessened by the modern barrier. Connor, knowing her so well, had surprised her by beginning the project while she was at work yesterday. He was constantly doing stuff like that—sensing her desires and working to make them reality. It was one of many, many things she loved about him.

As she watched, Justin came into view, also shirtless. He handed Connor another screw and then Connor handed him the drill. With endless patience, her dream lover slipped safety glasses over her son's eyes and taught him how to use the cordless drill. Justin finished securing the rest of the board by himself. Then he stepped back to admire his handiwork with pride, transforming his youthful features.

Stacey's chest tightened with the effort required to contain her love. Her eyes watered and her nose began to run. She reached for a tissue and forced herself to take deep, even breaths. If she got too upset, her nose would bleed, a side effect of the mind-infusion that she didn't want Connor to worry about.

As if he sensed the weight of her stare, Connor lifted his head and caught sight of her. He grinned and waved. Collecting herself, Stacey stepped on the accelerator and approached the house, turning into the driveway and shutting off the engine. He was opening the door and helping her out before she even had time to get the keys out of the ignition.

"I missed you," he rumbled, tugging with just enough force to bring her flush against him. "And I love these scrubs."

She laughed, thinking he was silly but glad that he was. Personally, she thought she was a bit nutty herself, and it was fabulous to share her life with a man who complimented that part of her. "You say that about all my scrubs."

"Yeah, but these are my favorite. They're sexy."

With both brows raised, she glanced down at her clothing. "I'm doing something wrong if your idea of sexy is two cartoon dogs."

"Ah, but look at how the girl dog is batting those long lashes at the boy dog. *That's* romance."

Stacey shook her head and glanced up at him, basking in the warm, affectionate glow in his eyes. "Romance is sexy?"

"Damn straight," he murmured, before taking her mouth in a hard quick kiss. When he pulled away, his gaze was dark with desire. "I can't do more than kiss you with Justin around. Even that makes him queasy, he says."

"Tonight, you're mine," she said, swatting his ass.

"You betcha." Connor caught her hand and pulled her toward the house. "I have something to show you."

"Oh, yeah?"

Every time he "showed" her something, it blew her away. His search for the artifacts forced him to travel a lot, but he was always thinking of her while he was gone. She knew it because of how often he called and by how many gifts he brought back for her. She didn't know how he did it, but he managed to dole out his presents here and there over the far-too-short trips home. Stacey knew she wouldn't have the patience. But, she had to admit, his way was far more fun.

He led her through the living room and into the bedroom, closing the door behind them.

"What about Justin?" she reminded, feeling her blood heat regardless. Connor's idea of a quickie put any other man's sexual marathon in the pale. They'd once been heading out the door to take him to the airport when he decided he needed to say good-bye intimately . . . *again*. He'd dropped his carry-on, his pants, and her scrub bottoms in half a minute. Within five more he'd had her muffling orgasmic cries into the cushions of her sofa as he rode her fast and furious from behind.

"He's waiting for me." His smile made her tummy flip. "We're going to finish that side of the driveway before the sun sets."

Connor tossed her purse and keys onto the bed, then reached for the hem of her shirt and tugged it over her head. Immediately, he dove for the valley between her breasts and nuzzled there.

"Yum . . . You smell good," came his muffled praise.

"You're crazy."

"Seriously." He lifted his head and arched a brow. "You and your apple pie are the best smelling things in this stinky world."

Laughing, she ran her fingers through his thick hair. "The world isn't stinky."

"Who are you kidding?" He reached for her waistband and pulled her pants down, pausing a moment to admire his handiwork as she kicked out of her sneakers. "Now *that's* sexy."

"Better than cartoon dogs?" She batted her eyelashes at him.

Her body was in pretty good shape these days, considering the work out he gave her when he was home and the extra care she gave to her appearance when he was gone. She trusted him implicitly, knew he loved her with every centimeter of his big heart, saw the proof of his pent up longing and lust in his gaze the moment he caught sight of her in the airport. But she also never forgot that the man was otherworldly fine. He looked gorgeous for her, the least she could do was try to return the favor.

"Maybe," he said, with a roguish shrug.

Her mouth fell open in mock affront, and he reached around her and undid the clasp of her bra.

"Okay." His brogue deepened at the sight of her bare breasts. "*That's* definitely better than cartoon dogs."

"Well, that's something, I guess."

"But not *the* something," he teased, dropping to a crouch and taking her panties with him. Connor pressed a kiss to her pelvic bone and stood. "Come on."

With his hand at the small of her back, he directed her to the bathroom. There she found their new self-heating spa tub filled with steaming water and surrounded by unlit candles. A metal caddy tray traversed the distance from one side of the tub to the other and held a small crystal vase of stargazer lilies—her favorite flower—and a jauntily opened box of gourmet chocolates.

"Nice!" She whistled, mentally calculating days and dates in an effort to recall if she should be marking an anniversary or special occasion of some sort. She winced as pain lanced through her head and she instantly gave up. Now was not the time to have a nose bleed.

Who knew the human brain could only hold so much information before it exploded? Thank god, someone in the Twilight was keeping an eye on her. Lieutenant Wager had coerced her subconsciously into sleep-writing a note to herself one night when Connor was away.

I'm working on it. Hang in there.

P.S. Wow! Have you got lots of great stuff in here.

Whatever. Stacey just felt better knowing that someone was actively working to help her. Who knew what she'd do if she didn't have Wager? Connor would drive himself insane trying to fix it and she knew there was nothing he could do. Having eons of information in her cranium told her that much. They had to get the data out of her head somehow and only the Elite in the Twilight had the technology to do it.

"You like?" Connor asked, beaming.

"I like," she confirmed, turning to face him and rising to her tiptoes to kiss him. "What's the occasion?"

"That's the something."

"The bath isn't the something?"

"Nope." He held out his hand to her and helped her into the tub.

After she sank beneath the water with a hiss of pleasure, Connor picked up a conveniently located lighter and lit all the candles. Then he kissed her forehead and said, "I'll be back in a bit."

He left the room and Stacey lay there a moment, trying to figure out what he was up to. Her gaze drifted around the tub, her heart both full and light. She reached for a chocolate and paused, noting the folded slip of paper beneath the gold foil box. Curious, she pulled it out and opened it.

Application for Marriage License.

Stacey froze.

The groom's side of the information had been filled out in crisp, clear print.

She exhaled slowly and carefully, then broke out in a wide grin. Maybe some women dreamed of romantic declarations, tuxedos, and/or grand gestures. Connor's gesture worked for her, because it came from his heart. She knew he had trouble putting his feelings into words, but he had no trouble showing her how he felt. After a lifetime of smooth-talking men who lacked substance, she loved having a man who was capable of so much more than just pretty, meaningless phrases.

From outside, she could hear the low rumble of Connor's voice on the porch, probably explaining something to Justin. Stacey was endlessly amazed by Connor's desire to teach and his aptitude for it. It was a natural extension of his thoughtfulness. He liked to say that he was all brawn, but really, she thought he was all heart.

Sighing with contentment, she set the precious paper down carefully and began to wash; preparing her body for the long night of lovemaking she knew was ahead.

"Does that dreamy smile mean what I think it does?"

Turning her head, she found Connor lounging against the jamb with wet hair and a towel around his hips. The image reminded her of their first night together and set her pulse rate racing. She loved it when he got so hot for her he couldn't wait a minute longer to get inside her. From the tent his cock was making against the terrycloth, it looked like he was close to feeling that way now.

"Does this paper mean what I think it does?" she retorted with a cheeky wink.

"If you think it means that I love you and want to make you mine in every way, then yes. You've got it right."

"I want you." The husky note in her voice left no doubt about what she wanted. She couldn't help it. Whenever he said the word "love," her instinctual response was the desire to wrap around him. To hold him and be held by him. To feel his beautiful body straining as he fucked her hard and long. "Is it nine o'clock yet?"

His slow, sensual smile started a quiver low in her belly. "No. But Lyssa and Aidan just left with Justin. He's going to stay with them tonight." With a quick tug, Connor dropped the towel, revealing his magnificent cock. "By nine o'clock you'll be begging me to let you catch your breath."

"Oh yeah?" She licked her lips as he approached, twisting to come up onto her knees.

"Oh yeah," he confirmed, leaning over to hit the switch and turn on the jets.

They'd had to replace the old shower/bath when he'd moved in to accommodate his size. Connor had sold several artifacts to McDougal, which afforded them a sizeable nest egg. They could move to a bigger, more modern house, but none of them wanted to. Instead, they preferred to fix up their existing home.

Connor stepped into the tub and she stopped him. "Wait."

He tensed and when his cock swelled further, she knew he understood what she wanted.

"Baby . . ." There was an aching note in his voice that made her nipples hard. He *loved* it when she gave him head. Loved it in a way that made her love doing it to him. With Connor, the act made her so hot, she felt like she was melting.

She gripped his erection with dripping wet hands and pulled his upthrust cock down to her waiting mouth. Her tongue darted out and licked across the tiny hole at the tip and he shuddered violently.

"Stace," he breathed, his hands sliding through her water-slicked hair. "You'll kill me."

The smile she gave him was pure mischief. "Lucky you're immortal, eh?"

Opening her mouth, she sucked the thick crest just barely inside, her tongue flickering teasingly across the sensitive spot just underneath. Connor's powerful thighs quivered and she reached around with one hand and cupped his ass.

"Yes," he hissed, his hips rocking gently. "Your mouth is so hot . . . the way you lick my cock . . ."

If she could have smiled, she would have. She loved the way he praised her, the way his hands moved so gently over her scalp even in his passion. She redoubled her efforts to please him, sucking stronger, her fingers kneading into the firm cheek of his ass. Her head bobbed as she rode the pulsing length with her mouth, using his groans and guttural cries to guide her. She took him as deep as she could until he butted up against the narrowing of her throat.

"Fuck. Ah, fuck, that feels so damn good, Stace."

She pulled back, licking him, swirling around the cum-slicked head before caressing the length of him. Tracing each throbbing vein with the tip of her tongue. She cupped his balls and rolled them tenderly, then reached her finger back and massaged his perineum.

He gasped and cursed, swelling thicker. She moaned in pleasure, her pussy slick and hot just imagining that big cock plunging inside her.

"I'm going to come," he warned, fucking her mouth with mindless thrusts that he kept shallow by fisting the base.

She could pull back and let him ride her to the finish. He loved that, too, and wouldn't complain, but she wanted this. Wanted to feel him come apart in a way he only could when he wasn't half focused on her climax. She hummed a sound of encouragement and Connor growled.

"That's it," he crooned in his deep brogue. "Suck my cock, sweetheart. Make me come. I'm so close . . . *fuck* . . . just like that . . . *Stace!*"

Connor spurted hard and thick, his hoarse cries of release filling the bathroom in a sensual music she would never get tired of hearing. He yanked free and pulled her up, hitting her chest with a burst of semen before he pushed her bottom onto the edge of the tub and thrust inside her hungrily clenching pussy.

She cried out in startled pleasure, the feel of him pulsing inside her so delicious. He wrapped his big body around her and pressed his sweat misted forehead into the crook of her neck. "I love you."

"Connor." Stacey wrapped her arms around him and held him. "I love you, too, baby."

His chest twitched against hers, then vibrated deeply when he let the laughter out. "I'm centuries older than you, sweetheart."

"Semantics," she muttered, licking the taste of him off her lips.

"I learned a lot in my many years," he purred, straightening and rolling his hips. She gasped as ripples of pure heat spread from where he stroked inside her. "Like this."

He withdrew, then thrust shallowly. Then withdrew again and thrust deeply. Stacey writhed and slipped on the watery ledge of the tub. Connor grinned and pinned her hips down with his hands. "Feel good?"

Rocking in and out, he fucked her pussy with breathtaking strokes, knowing just where to concentrate in order to make her beg. He was branding her from the inside out with his heated length of rock hard cock. He hadn't diminished at all from his first orgasm. The man had unbelievable stamina. Thankfully, he'd hooked up with the right gal, because she took all that he had and then wanted . . .

". . . more," she urged, her nails digging into his skin.

"But you're so tight. I don't think you can take any more of me." His grin was pure male satisfaction.

Stacey tightened up everything inside her just to watch his eyes darken and his cheeks flush. "I can take you, big guy."

He pushed her backwards and set both hands on either side of her. "I don't have much leverage with my feet in a hot tub of bubbles."

"Excuses, excuses." She set her hands behind her and wrapped her legs around his hips. "Lucky for us, I've been working out."

Tightening her thigh muscles, she lifted her buttocks up, sliding herself onto his cock.

"Fuck," he breathed, his abs clenching tight. "That feels damn good."

She pouted. "I wanna come."

"Your wish is my command." Reaching between them, Connor placed his thumb over her clit and thrust his cock in slow, shallow digs. Circling. Rubbing.

"Yes," she whispered, enamored with the feel of being stretched to fit him. "Oh god, yes!"

Her climax shuddered through her and he whispered to her, as he always did, naughty words of encouragement that made her orgasm last.

"So beautiful. That sweet little cunt sucking on my

cock." Connor kept stroking through her grasping ripples. "I'm going to get you in bed and ride you the way I want to. Hard and deep."

"Do it," she sobbed, clinging to him as her body dissolved into bliss.

How they made it to the bed, she'd never know. She just remembered being cradled against a hard chest, a strong heart beating beneath her ear, and then cool softness beneath her damp back as he laid her on a bed of rose petals.

"Marry me," he said, slipping an antique emerald ring onto her finger. "Let me love you forever."

"Yes." She cried softly, arching beneath him as he slid inside her, joining with her.

Making them stronger. Together.

# Glossary

CHŌZUYA: A fountain at the entrance to the Jinja (Shinto shrine) where ladles provide the means for guests to cleanse themselves before entering the main temple complex.

HAIDEN: The only part of a Shinto shrine that is open to the general public.

HONDEN: In Shinto shrines, the *honden* is the most sacred area. This is usually closed to the general public.

SCLERA: The sclera is commonly known as "the white of the eye."

SHOJI: In traditional Japanese architecture, a *shôji* is a room divider or door consisting of washi (rice) paper over a wooden frame. Shoji doors are often designed to slide open, or fold in half, to conserve space that would be required by a swinging door. (*Wikipedia.com*)

TAZA: A cup

TORII GATE: The gate to a Shinto shrine (Jinja), the Torii designates holy ground. The Gate marks the gateway between the physical and spiritual worlds.

SYLVIA DAY is the best-selling, award-winning author of over a dozen novels. A wife and mother of two, she is a former Russian linguist for the U.S. Army Military Intelligence. Her books have been called "wonderful and passionate" by WNBC.com, "wickedly entertaining" by *Booklist*, and frequently garner Readers' Choice and Reviewers' Choice accolades. She is an EPPIE winner and a prestigious RITA® Award of Excellence finalist. Visit with her at *www.SylviaDay.com*

To learn more about the Dream Guardians™, visit *www.DreamGuardians.com*.